Edited by Douglas Glover

Best Canadian Stories
02

We acknowledge the support of the Canada Council for the Arts, the Ontario Arts Council and the Government of Canada through the Book Publishing Industry Development Program for our publishing activities.

"Blame Canada" by Don McNeill was originally published in *Descant*; "Family Furnishings" by Alice Munro first appeared in *The New Yorker* and is reprinted by permission of the William Morris Agency; "My White Planet" by Mark Jarman was first published in *Prism international*; "What Saffi Knows" by Carol Windley was originally published in *Event*; "The Irish Book of Beasts" by Bernice Friesen first appeared in *The New Quarterly* and was broadcast on CBC Radio's *Gallery*; "Comedian Tire" by Bill Gaston was first published in *Prism international* and is reprinted in *Mount Appetite*; "So Beautiful the Firemen Would Cry" by Ramona Dearing originally appeared in *Prairie Fire*.

The following magazines were consulted: *Antigonish Review, Blood & Aphorisms, Canadian Author, Canadian Fiction Magazine, The Canadian Forum, Capilano Review, Descant, Event, Fiddlehead, Geist, Grain, Malahat Review, New Orphic Review, New Quarterly, The New Yorker, Nimrod, Paragraph, Pottersfield Portfolio, Prairie Fire, Prism international, Quarry, Saturday Night* and *Windsor Review*.

ISBN 0 7780 1204 2 (hardcover)
ISBN 0 7780 1205 0 (softcover)
ISSN 0703 9476

ONTARIO ARTS COUNCIL
CONSEIL DES ARTS DE L'ONTARIO

Book design by Michael Macklem

Printed in Canada

PUBLISHED IN CANADA BY OBERON PRESS

Contributions for the thirty-third volume, published or unpublished, should be sent to Oberon Press, 400–350 Sparks Street, Ottawa, Ontario K1R 7S8 before 31 March, 2003. All manuscripts should enclose a stamped self-addressed envelope.

INTRODUCTION

Every one of these stories is a favourite of mine, but after I read Michael Winter's "Unmoved," I was really loath to give up the manuscript to the publisher because I wanted to keep it around the house all for myself. "Unmoved" is a plaint for lost love in the Newfoundland mode—lots of love, lots of booze, a stormy night overlooking St. John's in a blackout listening to Bach and reading Don DeLillo, and no hope but in the language itself: "Pray for me. Okay, just get on your knees and move your lips. I have loved you. You." But then I also found a new Alice Munro story in the New Yorker— "Family Furnishings"—which is about sexual secrets, hidden pregnancies and Ontario family funerals where you might just end up meeting a sister you never knew you had. Apparently less dense, less constructed than they used to be, Munro's newer stories seem almost to wander along, pulling language and plot out of air, until it seems impossible that she could bring all the threads into a formal unity. But at the last possible moment, Munro performs a little flourish with her fingers, the past comes slap against the present, and the story closes back on itself with perfect certainty.

I admire Mark Jarman's new story "My White Planet" for its madcap premise (naked woman floats half-alive into an apparently forgotten Arctic radar station) and its language. "Another dead pilot soars over us, air gone, precision machine on auto, fly till fuel drained, flying on fumes, vapours wavering like ghosts inside steel rivets." But I was equally astonished when I read the manuscript of P.K. Page's "Ex Libris," a marvel of whimsy, foreshortening, linguistic sleight of hand, and magical plotting, a compressed novel—what you might expect from a great poet. And I laughed out loud at Don McNeill's "Blame Canada"—Confederation seen from the point of view of one member of a Newfoundland Boy Scout troop apparently interested equally in merit badges and masturbation.

Bernice Friesen's novel excerpt is story-like enough for me, not to mention charming, funny and cunning. In "The Irish

7

Book of Beasts" she tells the delightful tale of an old priest obsessed with horticulture and a small boy who unwittingly damages one of his ancient trees. The brothers in charge connive sweetly not to punish the boy who already has a broken arm from falling out of the tree. But when the boy returns to his dormitory with his arm in a cast, everyone knows the truth: "'They broke his arm. *Jasus.* He broke a branch so they broke his arm.'" Bill Gaston's "Comedian Tire" isn't really funny at all, is only comic in the deepest truest sense, that is, in its depiction of the way the mundane (in this case, car repairs) is always imposing itself upon the tragic (an unloved and unlovable brother's death). "The comedy of bodies and cars breaking down, the junk that lives become." And Carol Windley's "What Saffi Knows" is eerie and uncomfortable— in all the best ways. It's the story of a girl who knows her next door neighbour is guilty of kidnapping, imprisoning and murdering a boy. Afraid to speak, she cannot save the boy and must live her life trying to come to terms with her complicity in this unholy secret.

Ramona Dearing's "So Beautiful the Firemen Would Cry" is a gently ironic tale of roommates, friendship, suicide and love, a comedy of suspicion and recognition that begins: "I started keeping my toothbrush in my underwear drawer after Beanie told me what she did to her last roommate." And the same tone of comic whimsy carries over into Caroline Adderson's "The Maternity Suite," a four-part (dis)harmony of sibling rivalry, convoluted sexuality, marauding cats, and comic misunderstanding—not to mention an hysterical pregnancy that sends all the characters spinning.

DOUGLAS GLOVER

Unmoved

Michael Winter

This all happened after he broke up with Lydia. He'd been
with Lydia Murphy for seven solid faithful years of fierce love.
There was a night they landed in Greece. On their way to
Kenya, where her parents were working. They deplaned in
Athens: you are to eat at the airport and sleep in an adjoining
hotel. But the food was English. It was a buffet in white and
grey. Lydia saw a bus. They changed money and got a ride
into the dark centre of Athens. It was some kind of Greek
mardi gras. Costumes, voluntary parades. They peered into a
small festive restaurant in the Plaka still decorated with
Christmas lights, whitewashed cement walls. There was a
flourish of ordering by Lydia. Octopus and small fried fish
called madeiras. There was dancing and a short man encour-
aged Lydia and she did and the short man bought them an
aluminum carafe of retsina. They walked under floodlit marble
and found an idle taxi in the dawn and they surrendered all of
their drachmas to the front passenger seat. There was sleep at
30,000 feet. Distant territory rolled under them in bands of
marble blue then serene desert, red clay and finally jokey green
that drenched the plastic airplane window as they descended
and met her parents with a hangover. It was moments like this
that made him think it was for the long haul.

But they'd broken the plate. Lydia wanted to fix it but he'd
given up. It's true, he told Maisie (their friend, who had had
the bright idea seven years before that they should go out, a
friend full of conviction—but conviction for its own merit,
something both Lydia and Gabriel discovered over the course
of seven years). He hadnt loved anyone the way he'd loved

Lydia. That sounds like a country song, Maisie said. But he meant it. He knew it as he lifted half the furniture out of their Toronto apartment. Wrenched. As true as you can be in the lines of a country song. Most of those songs contain an emotional truth. They just lack a certain irony. A broken heart is bereft of irony.

They had moved to Toronto from St. John's, driven there in a brown car Gabriel revived with riveted rocker panels and a quart of tractor paint. The body work was still tacky as they boarded the ferry. Lydia was going to film school and he would write a book. And three years later that book offered some success. It's true the success was due to Lydia. Gabriel had written a good book because of Lydia. Lydia was in the book and she had read drafts and cried and was angry with him, the things he noticed, but she was a good reader and she pushed him. There was a catalytic agent in her.

He was ready to hate Toronto. But he liked how air conditioners dripped in doorways, the smell of propane exhaust from taxis. Toronto was a movie that played out in front of you.

Then they broke up. There was the day I mentioned when he moved the furniture. He lifted up a night-table. There was a photograph of the night-table with a lamp on it, the photo was taped to the wall above the night-table with the very lamp. That was the kind of thing that was on the wall in that apartment. He looked at the photo as he moved the lamp and lifted the night-table. It felt like he was uprooting teeth. It was shifting objects in photographs. He was excavating someone's mouth. Or, it was his mouth, a mouth he shared with Lydia. Going at molars with a set of pliers. I am rooting around in the mouth that I've built with Lydia.

Lydia said, about two months later, You were so sad that day. I've never seen you so sad.

She thought he'd come back.

Lydia knew an important older actor. The actor said, He must be crazy.

Insane.

Yes, perhaps he's a little insane.

She asked Gabriel that. Do you think you might have lost your mind a little?

Gabriel thought about that. Lost your mind.

But he was stubborn and had decided the plate was busted. For Lydia his leaving was almost a ploy. I say ploy because ploys usually fail. And. He stayed away. The first night on his own. When the new walls were bare. When flat things leaned against the walls. When all he'd plugged in was the little radio with red digital numbers and he'd strung a Malaysian sarong over the window, pinned at the top with thumbtacks. He was excited. He knew he'd be okay. He was happy with the height of the ceiling. Nine feet.

He was writing and he taught as well. Gabriel was teaching at the University of Toronto. He was walking down the same hall that Northrop Frye had walked down. I have driven up from nowhereville and now I am Northrop Frye.

Maisie said, You forget. Youve been working hard for twelve years.

Gabriel had published a book. And now. Now it was paying off. There were articles, and there were parties and he was new and liked. When he taught he noticed the students were listening to him. He was impressing them. He realized he believed things, that he had opinions and he'd learned technique. He had a skill.

That's where he met Krista Blades. She had this hair. Black as a magpie's wing. Eight months later—when she knelt over him on the balls of her flexed feet—Gabriel said, When you first met me. What did you think.

Krista: That you had good shoes.

She had him pinned with her hands on his chest.

What.

Jesus I'm trying to come here.

You can't talk about. I'll. A note on that.

You wore solid shoes, okay? With a strong leather tongue.

Did you know I was attracted to you.

I had no idea.

Really.

And she shuddered and closed her eyes.

Krista: I thought you didnt like me.

I wanted more of your attention.

So you had no. What about now.

Gabriel: When now.
When I kissed you. When I sucked your cock.
When you my elbow.
Before that you didnt know? Interesting.
Up on the balls of her feet, how astronauts walk on the moon.

Krista Blades was in the class and took the next class as well. She worked in reinsurance and she had just bought into a condo development on College that wouldnt be finished for sixteen months. She had clicked through a virtual tour of her apartment. She drove to class in a '66 Plymouth Valiant. She wore this green top. She had the dyed black hair. The hair was a negative space. Gabriel had decided to teach everything he knew in eight classes. He divided it into eight. And after Christmas he would teach it again. But four of his students signed up. So he had to find eight new classes of material.

Krista had this shyness. She had this smallness and this tallness. She had this it was hard to judge the size of her.

What more can you say after youve said avoid the passive voice, use delay, dont forget dialogue, and think about psychic distance? And if you know what's coming next in a story, then youve already said it.

She had this smoke break thing.

Reinsurance is like where we insure the insurance companies.

When Gabriel moved out of Lydia's apartment. He was living with two men and a woman in a house near Dundas and Dovercourt. It was 400 a month, that's why he took it. The men were Ryerson students reading Russian film theory and the woman had a nameplate, Princess, on her bedroom door. The woman had an audition in a female equivalent to Boogie Nights, she said. She worked at Hooters and had a boyfriend with a white BMW. She was poring over sheets of paper in the kitchen. It's some hard, she said, to prepare for this bar exam.

Oh.

Gabriel realized he had judged her.

Yeah, she said. There are so many different kinds of drinks to memorize.

It was a good room and he could move out from Lydia.
Lydia said, Can you leave the paintings. They were paintings
he'd done. So he left them. He left a lot of things. All the
music, a German kitchen knife, an oiled salad bowl. There
were many things that seemed petty to take. But he missed
them. But did he miss the objects or what the objects represented, infused as they were with Lydia's life. He had visited
Lydia a couple of times and it pained him. To see the apartment and the things he'd left behind. How could she live
there.

He'd forgotten how much light was in the apartment.

He had not lived with strangers since before Lydia. Seven.
Years.

He taught and he wrote and there was Christmas back
home in St. John's and then he taught and wrote and taught
some more and didnt write and drank a bit and fucked
around. He had never fucked around and now he was fucking
around a lot. Maisie said you have a window. Youre allowed a
window.

Is this a window in time or space.

It's a time window.

Through e-mail he rented a house in St. John's. For the
summer. He kept his room in Toronto. He rented a house
with an early postal code. The postal code was A1A 1A3.
That's about the third house from the Atlantic. Until October. Until three days before he had to teach again in Toronto.
He was, as they say, dividing his time.

What he was was okay. He was not desperate. A first for
that, he thought. Alone on earth care of milky way.

He was e-mailing some of the students. They were forming
a writing group. To meet and read their work. And then the
move back to St. John's and some of them were e-mailing just
to keep in touch.

Then Krista Blades e-mailed. To say she was coming east with
a friend. To Halifax and maybe St. John's. She was following
this accordion player. Would Gabe be around.

Youre more than welcome, he said. If you guys need to
crash. I'll ask Spencer.

13

Gabriel asked about Spencer. And then realized. He knew of him. He'd never met Spencer, but he.

I've met, Gabriel wrote, Spencer's first girlfriend. Twelve years ago. In Greece.

I'll ask S about that.

There's a loft and you can have it, he tapped back. Gabriel kept looking at e-mails. He thought, fresh. That bit. That whole exchange there. A way to write.

We'll come for three days, Krista wrote.

They wanted to drive around. Maybe he had. Some time?

And so Gabriel looked forward to it. He marked it on his calendar. He made sure he had a calendar with squares large enough to write things like that in. To whom and when he'd posted letters. What day he'd paid the rent, his return airfare, income. When a wildflower arrived in the garden. He admired Thoreau. He liked how his name was almost thorough. Did that convince Thoreau. At all.

The garden was seeded by Gabriel and his four-year-old niece. So carrots were in a curved line that missed the drill. A tomato grew out of the compost heap. A tough green bush of potato, like tobacco, out of the rockery. Parable of seed sown in shallow soil.

Lydia came by. With a box from her parents' basement. The last of his stuff in Lydia's life. She was home, too. She looked very. Thin. Maisie said: Too thin, Gabe.

And he had done that.

Maisie: When Oliver left, I didnt lose a pound. Not a single pound.

Gabriel: What does that mean, that you never loved Oliver? or it's wrong for Lydia. To lose weight.

No, Lydia wouldnt come in. But she was friendly. It pained him. There was something. Inside the eyes. We still havent figured out the eyes. If a planet stares at you, does it weigh more. Why the hell dont we talk about the eyes. The box: a boxing trophy, early nails, a pack of cards, a travelling scrabble board. Things from before his life with Lydia. The time he'd met Astrid, Spencer's Astrid. It all made him wince with an anguish of possible lives and the realization that he was getting older. He was extinguishing good old natural selec-

14

tion maybe, twisting it out underfoot. What a fucking waste, that's what he thought. He didnt hate Lydia. I cannot bear to be reminded of the life I am rescinding. So it's true, he thought. We'd prefer to not know. To not be reminded. If I had. My way—all past lives would be obliterated. Their facts refused access. No gain entry. Permission ungranted. Statement printed out on modern-day equivalent to ticker tape: Gabriel English does not care to see evidence of possible lives flourishing or waning.

Krista Blades at midnight. The house so close to the road and it's a quiet road. But there is no Spencer. It is Krista and her girlfriend Lisa Noble. How did this happen. That these. Strangers were staying with him. They coasted up in a blue rent-a-car. He had the porch light on and, when he heard the car, he stood out there on the cold wood. He was barefoot. The wood made him realize that. Wood is trees. The car lurched and their lights sank off. Krista and Lisa slanted out. They had been drinking. They were drunk. Lisa had been driving. She is tall, a painter, a landscape painter. They were not polluted.

This is some spot, Lisa said. Youre like the last house on the hill. Like in the world.

Then, Hi hi I'm Lisa. Krista introduce me for god's sake.

Krista held his elbow and went right past him with that flank of black hair. It was Krista Blades all right. He remembered her now. Thing is. Lydia had light hair. So there was that, just contrast. Yes, he was looking for contrast. Except he'd never seen Krista drunk and that was kind of a pass, that holding of the elbow. This woman was being forward because she was shy. We often confuse shyness for authority and the decision not to say something. Saying something is unnecessary.

Gabriel showed them the house. He did the thing Lydia had once done. To the living-room he said, And this is the bathroom.

But this confused them. Though they knew to laugh.

You got anything to drink here?

He had two bottles of red wine and three beer.

Let's have the wine.

It was September and it was still warm. He said let's take it outside.

That's fine. That's fine.

You can't see much from the house. If the hill is a molar then the house was sunk in its crown. You walked up the edges to the cusp. And there. Is everything. A path along the tooth that dips to the harbour and the city. A pretty good view. Gabriel knew they were standing on blueberries.

It's kind of rough, Lisa said.

He'd known nine women since he'd broken up with Lydia. I've been keeping that from you. Nine. It was an average of one a month. And theyd all had poor balance. Had he known to appreciate Lydia's balance.

Just take my hand, he said.

And Lisa Noble took his hand. It was Gabriel and Krista but Lisa Noble was okay with getting in the way. He was glad she pushed into them. It was brave.

They drank the wine and then it came to the beer. Is that it, Lisa said.

Well there's vodka.

Holy frig.

There might be brandy.

He's got fucking vodka.

In the freezer.

Tonic does he have tonic.

Lisa's head in the fridge. He's got orange juice.

They turn up the stereo, playing music retrieved from the rent-a-car. There is a CD by Spencer. What is it, like zydeco.

Spencer's coming, Krista says. He's like on his way.

The best songs, Lisa says, are songs that mention an I and a you.

That is so so true, Gabriel says. And you, a landscape painter from Toronto.

Are you. Making fun of me.

I love the landscapes of Toronto. The vista is so something.

He is. Making fun of me.

They are delighted by the vodka. And the vodka yes. The

vodka is introduced to a new round of frozen orange juice diluted by professional frozen-orange-juice diluters. A water glass topped with orange and vodka and ice. Gets slunked over the carpet. It forms a blue snake with a tail of bloodless chunks. As if. Creeping out of two dimensions. Oh god oh god that's not good, Krista. It's okay, Lisa. It's okay, isnt it Gabe? Sure, sure it's just a rented carpet it's just industrial. Maybe scoop up that ice.

So. There was a lot of drinking. It was a heavy bout. They were putting in a good shift at the alcohol plant.

The girls as if a clothesline pulled them into the bathroom. And there is an emptiness, a quiet and the light under the door and then the door opens and they walk out concentrated, as if in a parade and a decision was made in the light of the bathroom mirror. They test the ladder to the loft.

In the morning a pair of sunglasses lying on the stove burner. Gabriel reads the temple, Italy. He thinks, That's a first. And is it surreal. In the fridge a clear baggie with hand cream smeared over a disposable camera, ziplocked tight. Or it could be mayonnaise. He thought hand cream because of the hand cream tubes. God how a lightbulb makes food happy. In the bathroom a pair of pants. He lifts them to eye level. On the pocket, Porn Star. The pants are not big enough. They are comic pants. Pants meant to represent a race at two-thirds scale. He remembers that early in the morning the word demise was used as a verb. He understands he is veering into wreckage. He knows that whatever Krista and Lisa want to do, he will do it. They wear pants like this. He holds them aloft and salutes them.

Kitchen and a click in the brain. He shunts on the water. Yes, that seems right. Water moving is the right answer. He grinds coffee and flicks on the maker. It is such a good idea to have a red light come on the flicker. He has no problem thinking of a time when he will lose his mind. The coffee information had almost receded into an oyster shell. Look at the weather. Get a newspaper. Go. The weather is a brain. What clouds do, that word attenuate. That will happen to the brain. A slow dissolve.

He walks down to the bright hotel for the free newspapers. His head is of a different air pressure. He can feel the resistance to diffusion. He is in his slippers. Shag writing and drift.

For five days he says yes to them. Yes camp and yes swim and yes visit towns with funny names. Yes Dildo. He has the receipts. After theyre gone he adds them. If you round up, 700 dollars of booze. Krista says never mind Spence, never mind he's fucking around he's. The fuck king.

They see gannets mating, a diving puffin, a sunrise. Look at that bitch move, Lisa says, to the sun. Has he ever heard the sun called a bitch. And as they walk up a hill back to the car, Tighten your glutes. They hunt down a forlorn out-of-season humpback and Krista squeals. The green flukes. He knows it's wrong to think that she squealed, but there is no other word for it. Does he find it attractive. That's what Maisie asked afterwards. Well, there are many moments like this, he said to Maisie. Just as there were images he still held of Lydia or Spencer's first girlfriend or his own first girlfriend Doris, though when those scenes occurred he was careful, almost possessed with an urgency, to write them down. Whereas now they were just happening to him, they were a wash with less effect. Maisie: You are unmoved.

When Spencer arrived it was their last day. Gabriel loved him. You could not not. It was the hair, it was the doomed whiff. It was the red accordion he lugged under his arm. The unearned physical side. The salute to talent born, not made. There was the unconscious angle of his limbs as he smoked in a chair. And while Spencer and Krista were upstairs in the loft, Gabriel decided on Lisa. And Lisa Noble accepted it. I am accepting drift. I am crossing over.

They slept and Lisa Noble pushed him away. She needed room. She was sleeping with Gabriel for the entertainment value. There was exercise in the sex. She was working out. It was doing situps the thing they were doing, it was aerobics. Gabriel went to the bathroom but the light was on. And then it was Spencer. Spencer was holding a belt. He said, I was just thinking of hanging myself.

Gabriel looked at his neck. He decided to listen to the next thing Spencer said. He could hear the jingle of the buckle. Spencer said, I'm okay now. And then he moved to the side. Did this happen. It happened.

They drove to Cape Spear. Lisa, they decided, the least drunk. Gabriel snapped on his seatbelt. His one concession to caring. He did it for the sake of his niece. He did it for Maisie. I do this for the ones I love. He did not tell Lisa to slow down. He knew they would go off the road. Four percent of him willed it. The turn in the hill is tight, the camber all wrong for the gradient. It's a shittily designed road and he knows it. A veering, a shift of weight. The floor under Gabriel's feet jars hard through a ditch. The car slumps. A jerk in their seats and the dark silence of pre-dawn. Gabriel turns to Spencer: Do you remember me?

Spencer: There were postcards. And I knew I was on waivers. Astrid fucking loved you man.

They sat there thinking about the ones that have left them.

Astrid, married. Two children now. Gabriel had visited her. He had read from the book in Ottawa. Where she lived with Alfred Tzanis and his permanent collection at the National Gallery. What a guy. And here I am sitting in the dark in a dead car. Alfred Tzanis was often on loan to other galleries. What was it there's a name for it. Not a restorer.

Lisa jerked the steering into park and sank back on her bucket seat. The dashboard had gorgeous new lights. It was a new cheap car. It would have a solid spare.

Gabriel found the jack. You need a hand, mate. No fuck no. Just good, a swig. Through the window Spencer passes out the bourbon. Then under the wheel well, the car hunched up, the hand brake on, you sure it's on. Lurching with the three of them—Krista, Lisa and Spencer and a bottle of Kentucky bourbon and a red accordion, the wheel well rocking over Gabriel's head, the glint of a hubcap's brushed aluminum. This head. This head my friend is the softest, smartest thing anywhere in the vicinity of this meaty ton of wheel well. I am plastered under a car full of strangers singing sea shanties.

I just need that bourbon again Mr Gabriel English.

Gabriel thought it had come to this and could he have predicted it. But so what about predicting. Predicting is overrated. Big fucking deal.

He followed them to the airport in his own shitbox. In a week he'd park the shitbox at Maisie's and head back to Toronto. Gabriel knew he had been loved and could be loved. But that was in reference to Lydia. It had taken the nine months to conclude that. There was the ride back to the house when you often conclude things. He decided to be open.
I guess I dont mind, he said to the shitbox windshield. Then, Good.
He counted the wildflowers. There was something called an arrow-leaved tearthumb. Every wildflower looked exactly like its photograph. So what was wild about them.
When he opened the door he was surprised. The house was neat. They had cleaned up.

His last night. The tail of a hurricane. The house was shaking. It was cracking. There were major beam splinters happening above his head. It was midnight. In fourteen hours he'd be in Toronto. He would accept a ride in the '66 Valiant and take a tour of Krista Blade's virtual apartment—she had it on CD-ROM. He'd see Lisa Noble at a Power Plant show where they'd shake hands with the Prince of Wales. Gabriel would miss the east coast winter when every storm in the Gulf of Mexico smacked into the forehead of Newfoundland. The winter Maisie lost her sense of humour. He was teaching and working on a novel. But this last night he was in his rented Newfoundland bed, getting his money's worth, listening to the storm gather interest. A tongue of wind trapped in the chimney flue. He decided. He chose. A jaunt up Signal Hill in the shitbox. He took the whiskey Spencer had left him, and Don DeLillo's play, *Valparaiso*. Loaned to him by Maisie. He cradled the bottle between his thighs, the tumbler with two cubes up on the dash. The fog. Wind bucking the car. Steaming up, he was looking through those two little arcs the defog manages to muster. He twisted the radio's on knob. It was a Bach cello suite. That first one, the epitome of the cliché male orgasm. And that's what drove him up the hill.

He cut the engine. There was an oblong of St. John's harbour kind of blurry in the wind and rain. Then he got down to work. He switched on the dome light. He wondered how many watts that was. Maybe twelve. Pour a finger. Turn off Bach, bye Bach. Open DeLillo. God he's good, he's really good. Modern. Just modern is the word. It decides things for you, that kind of writing.

The car rocked on its wheel wells. That's half a ton, lurching.

He got to page 79, then decided. He was being deliberate. Undo seatbelt, swing door open. Drenched. He walked around the Marconi tower. He circled this most solid of buildings. Saw the car. The car creaking on its axles in the wind. He'd left the dome light on. Through the wet window Spencer's shiny red button accordion. He'd forgotten his accordion. And Gabriel would have to play it at the x-ray machine in the Departures lounge. To prove it was not a bomb. The scene that ended his summer in St. John's.

There was a spank of black and the city went down. The power failure began in the north and trickled down to the harbour. So the city vanished. It was there now it did not exist. The only light from ships docked at the apron. Oh you vehicles of independence. Was that it then. Was this the end. You needed light. You needed to be a goddam ship with personal reserves.

He got in the car.

He had his twelve watts of dome light. Keeper of the flame I am. Gabriel switched on the headlights. This was all right. Light just soaking out of me. He drove home and paused with the lights on. Then shut them down. He knew he had them, in case. It was good to know. If they could make a car with a bed in it. The house black and a search in drawers for candles, for waxy things. A force ripping into the profile of the house. Just socking it. There was water dribbling through a ceiling light fixture. That can't be good. He wanted to find a bible. He wanted to name the allusion.

Pray for me. Okay, just get on your knees and move your lips. I have loved you. You.

21

Blame Canada

Don McNeill

Back in the year we joined Canada, Vern Tibbo was the best in our class. He was the best student, the best hockey player, the best liked, the best everything; he always had the best bike—he was the first one to get gears—and until that summer he was also my best friend.

The year before, the unholy row about Canada came right into our classroom. Our Grade 8 teacher, Mr. Fizzard, was part of Joey Smallwood's Confederation team, and whenever the opposition sound trucks of the Responsible Government League drove by our school, blaring their call for a return to national independence through our classroom window, he would stride over, raise the sash, hawk up a good one and let her go. For weeks we wrote DONT VOTE CONFEDER-ATION on the blackboard every morning, and for weeks Mr. Fizzard would wipe it off first thing, without a word, when he came in. Finally we switched to VOTE RESPONSIBLE GOVERMENT to see what that would do. Mr. Fizzard looked at it the first morning, picked up the chalk and put an N between the R and the M, then sat on the edge of his desk and looked out at us. "Now that," he said, jerking his thumb back at the writing on the board, "is the most stupid fucking thing a man could do. Can you tell me why Tibbo?"

You could hear the sharp intake of air in the room, the gasps, and a few nervous titters among us boys (we were not co-ed in the classroom in Newfoundland in the late nineteen-forties). But we'd finally got to him.

Vern shook his big curly head slowly, playing it safe. "No sir, I can't."

22

"So much for the class brain," Mr. Fizzard said, turning to me. "How about your bosom buddy, the wit Fisterre?"

"I haven't got a fucking clue, sir," I said.

Whoops of laughter shot round the room like the hoots of the sealing ships bouncing off the harbor hills when they left for the ice in March. I'd brought down the house and I basked in the moment, seeking out Vern's wry smile, the way he would look at me, shaking his head in disbelief. *What won't you do for attention Luke?* For him my answer was nothing, although my risk at school and at home in this case wasn't so big. Mr. Fizzard couldn't report me for foul language because there were 30 boys who would swear he'd used the F word first; also when word of my "wit" spread throughout the school and to my older brother, Jack, he was more likely to try to blackmail me for part of my allowance than rat on me to our sainted mother, the terrible swift sword of moral wrath in our household. I could promise Jack payment and then keep defaulting every week until I had something on him to cancel out the debt, like the next time he skipped music lessons with Mr. Crawford, the church organist and choirmaster for whom I was still the lead boy soprano, and from whom I extorted 50¢ a month, twice as much as any other choirboy got.

Vern, as I said, had a big head with soft curly brown hair, slightly protruding ears, calm hazel eyes and a very square set of shoulders. He was good with his hands and we made mighty constructions with our combined Meccano sets. His father was an electrician and Vern had learned how to put little electric motors into our works to operate pulleys, raise and lower platforms, open and close bridges. We did most of this play at Vern's house out at the western edge of the city. Some nights on weekends I would stay over and sleep with Vern, after Mrs. Tibbo called to check with my mother—they had known each other since they were children, both their families being from the old French fishing villages in Fortune Bay. Sometimes it was vice versa at our house in the city after Scouts on Friday night when Vern would have a long ride home on his bike. But I preferred Vern's place. For one thing, out there I wouldn't have to share Vern with anyone, especially not with Gary Greeley, a boy in our class at school who

23

was also in the same scout troop, the 3rd St. John's. On Friday nights, Gary hung about us on our way home, circling round on his bike, showing off. We went everywhere on our bikes before the snow came, and my big embarrassment was that I had a girl's bike, bought by my father secondhand. I always mounted it like a boy's bike and proclaimed that I didn't need a cross bar. "I got my own right here," I would boast. "Yeah! Let's see it!" Gary once said in reply, and I told him it would cost him five dollars. Not even Gary was going to pay that much to see my cock, though he did seem to have more money than the rest of us. When we stopped at Doyle's store for Pepsis after Scouts he would offer to buy us date squares. I knew it was Vern he was buying for. Gary never paid any attention to me during the week.

The reason Vern was such a good hockey player was that he had a pond right next door to his house. He and his younger brother, Bumby, were out there on skates the moment it froze hard enough to hold their weight. On weekends and holidays in winter, I would leave our house first thing in the morning, my old hand-me-down skates from Jack and a battered hockey stick over my shoulder, and head out for Tibbo's pond. I tried hard at hockey, but I wasn't very good. What I really looked forward to was when darkness came and we were warm and cosy in Vern's house, down on the floor with our Meccano constructions. At Xmas I was given a choice of new skates or more Meccano—a new bike was out of the question. A few days after, when Mrs. Tibbo asked me what I'd got and I told her more Meccano, she raised her eyebrows and said, "I thought you might be growing out of that by now." Vern had got a new bike with gears.

Our school's junior hockey team was chosen in January and I didn't make it. Of course, Vern made it, and so did Gary Greeley. I was surprised when Gary made it. I thought I could skate as well as he did. He could hardly skate at all. But all those Saturdays when I was out at Vern's pond, Gary was playing shinny on the street and he was very good with his stick, cunning and quick and dirty in a mob around the goal. I started calling him "Hooks." I put the word around that I'd

24

been told I didn't make the team because I was still too young to be eligible. I was younger, it was true, the youngest boy in our class by more than a year. The story my mother told was that when Jack, two and a half years older than me, went off to school, I had cried and cried so hard that the only way they could get me to stop was to send me to school too, with the school's proviso that I spend two years in kindergarten. But even then I was a year too soon for my age group. I never believed the story because I couldn't believe that I could miss Jack that much.

I went to all the games and cheered Vern on, but I enjoyed belittling Gary's goal-scoring in my play-by-play commentary. "The puck goes in to "Hooks" Greeley again. He has it! ...He has it!...He still has it!...He hasn't moved!...He still has it!...He can't move!...My God! He scores!" I wormed my way into the dressing-room after the games and praised Vern. And just like after Scouts, we went off for Pepsi's together to Doyle's where old Dick always served us like we were one customer—"What can I get for Vern-'n-Luke?"

My father liked to say that April Fool's Day, 1949, was the day we joined Canada—officially, it was one minute *before* midnight on March 31st—and on that day he wore a black armband to work. Mr. Fizzard wore a white carnation in his lapel and a grin a yard wide: he was to be a Minister in Joey's new government. Confederation with Canada meant different things to different people, but for the "common man," my father's favourite person, it meant money. My father's favourite kind of politician was one who had the "common touch," but he couldn't credit Joey with having it—which he did in abundance—because Joey was a Townie upstart, as common as himself, a man he'd known in school as a scrawny dropout nicknamed Splits who had succeeded in politics only by conning votes from the dumb baymen with the promise of money for making babies and not fishing. "See, It's true!" he said, outraged when I told him three days after Confederation that Bumby Tibbo reported that he was hanging around outside Doyle's when one of the corner boys, "Gull" McGuffy, came running up to his fellow unemployed buddies and said in breathless, incredulous gasps, "B'ys...you gotta get up...to Buckmaster's Field...they're giving away...*money*!" (McGuffy, nicknamed the "Gull" because he was a renowned scavenger, was on to a good thing from the start: he would one day scoop up the job of Lieutenant-Governor of the Province.)

For me and Vern and the other boys in the 3rd St. John's, the act of Confederation meant one big thing—a trip to Ottawa that summer as part of the first Newfoundland contingent ever to attend Canada's National Boy Scout Jamboree. Scouts from each city troop would be selected, and the scramble began to pile up merit badges. The 3rd St. John's had a log cabin out near Logy Bay, and when the snows started to melt we headed out there on our bikes on weekends to hone our skills at cooking, rope-knotting, wood-carving, weaving, rock-climbing, firelighting, or anything else that could mean another badge to be sewn on our shirtsleeves, by ourselves not our mothers. There were, of course, no merit badges for farting, belching or pissing the furthest. Nor for the jerk-off contests that seemed to me to sprout up out of nowhere that Spring.

Our cabin was on the shore of a pond, a forested hillside rising behind. The other side of the pond was cleared farmland, with a farmhouse owned by a family named Heal. My parents were worried about me going out to the cabin because Jack had reported that an Assistant Scoutmaster, a man named Wilf Luffton, was queer. Watch out for Wilf, Jack and the older scouts warned their patrols, and whatever you do, don't go out driving with him. Luffton liked to offer boys the chance to drive his car and when your hands were busy on the wheel, his hands were all over you. My father was outraged by Jack's news. He thought all Scoutmasters were pansies until proven otherwise. Ours, Bill Atkinson, was deemed okay because he had the hots for Betty Heal. I was famous for my response to the cry of "Where's Atkinson?" from a paddler coming up the pond. "He's over the Heal's and far away," I yelled back. (I guess you had to be there.) Anyway, my father and the other parents got on to Atkinson about Luffton. Gay meant a happy person back then, which Luffton wasn't when Atkinson had to tell him he couldn't stay in the troop anymore. Queer was what we called him, or a fruit, but my father, a generation earlier than us, called him a pansy, which is a flower. So names, I learned, can mean different things to different people at different times. (Or is it that people can mean different things by the way they use names, like later in Quebec when one man's terrorist was another man's freedom fighter.)

Vern and I were in the same patrol, the Loons, and Jack was our Patrol Leader, which I didn't like at all. But it was better than having Gary Greeley be a Loon. Out at the cabin, we were assigned to bunk-rooms by patrol. Vern and I had our sleeping-bags side by side and we could talk in the night until Jack told us to shut up and go to sleep.

On a sunny Saturday afternoon in late May, Vern and I were practising our cooking—scorched, doughy rolls, were the best result so far—when we heard raucous laughter in the woods nearby. Each patrol had a lean-to in the woods near the cabin, each with a stone fireplace for cooking, and we competed in bread-cooking contests. The laughter came from the direction of the Owls Patrol and we crept over there to see what was going on. At the edge of the clearing we both stood up, so struck with what we saw that we didn't bother to conceal ourselves anymore.

Gary Greeley and another boy named "Goat" Gillingford lay side by side on a tarp in their lean-to, pants down around their knees. They were jerking off. Their eyes were closed, their faces tensely strained in concentration and effort. Other boys stood around watching, joking, calling out encouragement. One of them, Stink Tucker, held a watch. It was some kind of competition.

"Ahhhhhh!" Greeley suddenly cried out, white gobs of spunk spurting from his cock.

"Forty-two seconds!" Stink shouted.

I'd never seen anything like it before. I looked at Vern. He was grinning. Had he done this before? I hadn't. What did I know? That when you were *doing it* with girls and they crossed their legs on you they could clamp your cock between two bones and you'd have to go to hospital to get it loose or maybe have it cut off, *that's* what I knew! The language, of course, I knew and used—*hard-on, jerking off, spunk, fucking*—but the words had no passionate charge attached to them. They didn't live for me. They were just words, used for jokes, or for a kind of bravado. I didn't *jerk off* or *fuck* or *do it* because I had not yet any biological urge to do it.

With a bleat and a burst of spunk, Goat Gillingford finished off a moment later.

"Forty-seven seconds," Stink announced. "Gary wins by five seconds."

They saw us now and Gary called out, "Hey! Here's some Loon competition...Vern 'n Luke. Bet you guys can't beat us!"

Others chimed in. "Yeah! Let's see the Loons do it!"

Vern looked at me. "Come on, let's do it."

"You done this before?"

"Yeah, sure, with Bumby." Vern paused, cocking his head slightly to the side as he looked at me. "You haven't?"

"I don't know...I mean...Yeah, sure!...But not with Jack."

And why not with Jack? I was thinking. That bastard! Why hadn't he told me about this, showed me how to do it? Wasn't that what big brothers were for?

"So what," said Vern. "Let's go!"

We lay down side by side on the tarp. I watched from the corner of my eye what Vern did and followed, unzipping myself and pushing down my pants. My cock , I thought, was regular size, not so big, not so small, somewhat like most of the others I'd seen during the pissing contests. I grasped myself and started the motion, praying I would get a hard-on. But that's all there was—nothing but motion. I didn't feel a thing, except foolish, and a growing fear of being laughed at.

I turned my head and glanced at Vern. His eyes were squinched shut, his teeth bared, and he was pumping away for all he was worth. What was he seeing behind those squinched eyes? It was supposed to be girls. But who? Betty Heal? I closed my eyes and thought of her *doing it* with Bill Atkinson, or what I thought *doing it* would look like. I felt nothing. I thought about Nancy Parsons, one of the girls from the female side of our school. Some of the boys, including Vern and a girl named Shirley Brooks, were pairing off after school and I felt I had to go along, so I chose to walk home with Nancy because one of the other girls had whispered to me, "Nancy thinks you're cute." Outside her house I talked a blue streak, not knowing what else to do. She said my singing in the church service on the radio on Sunday was cute.

"Luke is thinking about Sophie Miller."

I recognized Gary's voice, him getting a big laugh with that one. Ms. Sophie Miller was our Latin teacher—*duco, ducis, duCUNT*, we'd chant, snickering behind our hands. Ms. Miller was old, short, dumpy, and had very bad breath.

I opened my eyes and looked at Gary.

"Not after she just finished with you," I said.

And the laugh I got was much louder than his, which saved me and almost drowned out Vern's groan as he came.

"Thirty-eight seconds!" Stink shouted. "Vern's the best."

At home, I lit into Jack for not showing me how to jerk off. But it wasn't something you could just show somebody, Jack said, you had to want to do it. Show me, I insisted. And he did it lying on his bed, holding up a magazine advertisement of a woman modelling underwear. I took the magazine and went at it for minutes, but nothing happened, except I wanted to piss.

"You just gotta keep trying," Jack said. "It'll come."

This was one of those periods in life when time seems infinite. What did a couple of months matter, a year even, before I was as horny as the rest of them? For me it mattered a lot. Vern could do something I couldn't share. I felt alone, trapped in a hopeless eternity, waiting for a time that I thought would never arrive.

When the selection for Ottawa was announced, I was so relieved I'd made it. So did Vern, and my brother Jack, of course, him being a King Scout now with more merit badges than anybody else in any troop in the city, and the more unbearable because of it. But so did Gary Greeley.

We were to be integrated with the scouts selected from other troops and reorganized into new patrols, and for this purpose, among other things, we all went off to camp for two weeks when school ended in June. The camp was at a place called The Motion. It was on the Marine Drive, a coastal road out of the city, not far from Logy Bay. East of it was Ireland and fog, which rolled in at some time everyday, sometimes so thick you couldn't see across the wide green field sloping down to the sea around which our tents were pitched. Our great leader was Louis Molloy, the Chief Boy Scout of the country, now demoted to a Province, the tenth Province of Canada, an Atlantic province dubbed "Atlantis" by my father, a lost nation. Canada was led at the time by Prime Minister Louis St. Laurent, known popularly as "Uncle" Louis. (The affectionate title was bestowed on him, I learned later, by Liberal Party flacks who wanted to warm up the austere image of a remote corporate lawyer from Quebec). Naturally, Louis Molloy became our Uncle Louis.

Every morning before breakfast, Uncle Louis would emerge from his tent in the buff to do his exercises. He had a large pot belly, a big dick, and a huge set of balls, and they all flopped up and down when he did his jumping jacks. Uncle Louis loved to march, I mean really march, arms swinging up parallel to the ground, like in the British army in which he had served with Monty in North Africa. In Ottawa, we were told, the scouts from each of the Provinces would be expected to put on a show. Our show, Uncle Louis had decided, would be to march and sing. We'd carry five-foot wooden staves instead of rifles, but there'd be no tossing and twirling like with a fancy drill team. We'd march like infantry. And sing Newfie songs. And for this purpose we were organized not in patrols but in platoons, six platoons in all, eighteen scouts per platoon, three tents of six scouts each per platoon, plus a command tent for Uncle Louis and his staff officers, and a huge mess tent. The Pentagon couldn't have done better.

All this was announced to us on the morning of the first day and I was antsy when it came time to pick platoons. I had to be with Vern. We were still best friends, I thought, but ever since the masturbating with Gary Greeley I had been uneasy, worried, yes, even jealous. I got Vern to come with me to see Bill Atkinson, who would be one of the platoon leaders. "We gotta be together," I said. And Atkinson looked from me to Vern and back to me and nodded and said that he would see what he could do. Imagine my relief when, a short while later, I learned that Vern and I would be in Atkinson's platoon *and* in the same tent.

By the afternoon of the first day we got it pitched, Bell Tent #2, Platoon #5. We had camp cots and I made sure mine was next to Vern's. Three of the other boys in the tent were from different troops, while our sixth occupant, Stink Tucker of the 3rd St. John's, we already knew.

"Anybody seen Stink?" I asked of nobody in particular.

And Stink stuck his head in through the tent flap at that moment and said, "Hey Vern, can I talk to you?"

Vern went out the flap and I followed.

Outside was Gary Greeley. "Stink has got a buddy in my tent," Gary said to Vern. "Okay with you if him and me switch and I come over here?"

Vern shrugged, and we both answered as if in one breath.

"Sure," he said.

"NO!" I shouted.

And before I knew what I was doing I struck out at Gary, climbing aboard him, cursing him and swinging wildly, and we went down in a heap.

Bill Atkinson had us apart in a minute, demanding to know what had happened. Gary and Stink and I said nothing and Atkinson looked to Vern.

"Gary asked me if he could switch tents and I said sure," Vern said, "but Luke got really angry...."

"Does it matter to you?" Atkinson asked Vern.

Vern shrugged...*What else!* "It really seems to matter to Luke," he said, "so I guess it's better if he and Gary are apart for now."

Atkinson nodded. "That's the answer then."

After dinner Jack took me down to the edge of the field overlooking the sea. The long Atlantic rollers crashed on the rocks below. The days were long and the sun was just setting, casting an eerie pink glow in the bank of fog far out on the eastern horizon.

"You know you're too young for this trip," Jack said.

31

"You're supposed to be at least fourteen and the only reason you're being allowed to go is because you're such a crybaby and Mom knows I'm here to look after you."

"I can look after myself," I said.

"Yeah? Then grow up and do it. No more fighting. Okay?"

I looked out at the pink fog bank, raised my hands and cupped them at my mouth to form a megaphone.

"Gary Greeley is an arsehole!" I shouted over the sea to Ireland.

There is in our culture no age for boys more idiotic than the age of "self-abuse," so-called by Victorians obsessed with the evils of masturbation. The tyranny of the red hand of shame! An age of wrestling and groping, girl-gawking, and furtively jerking off under the sheets, behind bathroom doors, in your sleeping-bag, wherever. And the inane jokes! Look! You got hairs on your palm! Not men, yet no longer really boys, boasting but bewildered, rambunctious yet shy, libidos unfocused yet raging for release like tightly cinched bulls at a rodeo, imagine now a train load of such tormented and tormenting animals. And imagine me, out on the edge of this bubbling pool of testosterone, jealous whenever I watched Gary grab for Vern's crotch in the aisle of our car, toiling away with myself in my top bunk above Vern as we rolled down the tracks in the dark of night, hoping against hope for some result. I wasn't shamed by "self-abuse," I was shamed because I couldn't do it.

I wanted to belong!

The trip to Ottawa took us four days. The narrow-gauge Bullet across the island accounted for one of them, and then came the great moment when we stepped ashore in our new country—Canada. And it really did look new to us. Sort of store-made. For one thing, the towns we passed through looked so tame, all orderly and right-angled, not that wild scattered look of our towns, the houses and shops flung down helter-skelter and the roads following old footpaths, always winding away from the sea, as if the first man ashore had staggered about drunk and the rest had just followed. The Canadian boy scouts our special train picked up along the way in Nova Scotia and New Brunswick were different too. For one thing, our uniforms were all khaki, shirts and shorts, but theirs were green and blue and some khaki; also they were overly polite and friendly, like somebody had told them that we didn't have much, were less fortunate than them, and to be kind. More than once we were asked about Eskimos, did we live among them. "Oh yeah," I said with bland-faced sincerity to a boy from Moncton. "We have two-storey igloos." There *was* something we *did* have, though, something that they treasured: our sealskin hat-bands, made especially for the Jamboree.

We crossed into Quebec and in Rivière-du-Loup on the evening of the third day, our leader ran across the crowded platform and bought a bunch of bricks of ice cream for us. "Uncle Louis, Uncle Louis, Uncle Louis," we chanted, filling the open windows on the platform side of the train. The crowd looked at us as if we were crazy, and some people even hissed. Why, we wondered? (I didn't know then that in this province the real Uncle Louis was considered by some to be *anglifié* and a *vendu*. Talk about foreshadowing! Here it was, only the third night of my entry into my new country, and already I'd met some people who wanted to get out!) Almost all our popular culture up to then had been American and all our history English history—I could do the Kings backwards. We'd had no Canadian history and the only thing I knew about French Canadian culture was "Johnny Corteau," a poem which Mr. Fizzard recited in class:

Johnny Corteau of de river,
Johnny Corteau of de hill,
He was de boy who could jomp and run,
He was de boy who could shoot de gun.

Oh yes! I also knew that Wolfe had beat Montcalm on the Plains of Abraham!

On the fourth day we leapt out of Quebec and rattled onto the trestle across the Ottawa River. All hands were at the windows, gawking at the Parliament buildings clustered on the cliff on the far side. "There she is!" declared Uncle Louis. "That's your famous Peace Tower." The thing stuck up like a giant poker with the old Red Ensign, Canada's flag at that time, flying off the top. "She's almost as big as Uncle Louis's cock," I said to the boys at my window. Privately, I was impressed. Parliament Hill looked to me a lot more important than the old Colonial Building back in St. John's. So much stone!

On the other side of the river we went into a tunnel and in less than minute emerged into a grand station. I'd never seen anything like it before, except in the movies, a great booming hall with a ceiling practically out of sight it was so high. (This station wasn't torn down like so many others in later years when train travel faded, but became a conference centre, a meeting place where Canadians continue to this day their ceaseless debate about who they are, their words echoing off in the vast space above their heads.) We were bussed straight through the city so we didn't get to see much of it for a few days. But one thing I did notice right away out the bus window was that there was no wood, I mean none of the houses or other buildings were built with wood. It was all stone and brick which made it seem cold and lifeless somehow.

Our camp was set up on the bank of the Ottawa River, and I got a better look now at the big, brown, sluggish body of water, bigger than any river I'd ever seen, I mean one that flowed between two banks—the St. Lawrence that we'd crossed back at Rivière-du-Loup was more like one of the bays back home. The campsite was already prepared for us. The latrines were real toilets, in low brick buildings which also had washrooms and showers. The tents were already up, aligned in neat rows like streets—they even had numbers—and divided into ten sections, one for each province, so some were bigger than others. The sections were placed along the four sides of a square, leaving a big meeting place in the middle; the order of placement around the square was the same as in which the provinces were stretched out across the country. So we, being the new Newfie boy at the far end of her, were rafted against Nova Scotia on one side and, just like we'd scooted underneath the whole shebang and lashed her all

34

together, were tied up to British Columbia on the other side, if you see what I mean.

Anyway, it seemed word of our sealskin hat-bands had spread rapidly from the Nova Scotia boys and the rest of the Maritime crowd. The scouts from British Columbia were coming over in droves to look at them and were offering to trade for them before we even got into our tents. When this sort of thing had started on the train in Nova Scotia, Uncle Louis had warned us that any boy who traded his hat-band before the last day of the Jamboree would be sent straight home. Even so, some of us were taking orders in advance, so to speak. But I decided to wait, gambling that as we were so few and they so many, the price would have to go up as the end got near.

My assigned tent was Newfoundland #7. So was Vern's, of course—we'd been told that we would keep the same groups that we'd had at The Motion. I had sat beside Vern on the bus, but now, what with all the hullabaloo going on in the narrow little streets, sorting ourselves out, meeting new boys and so on, I'd lost track of him. I went inside the tent with my duffel bag. He wasn't there. I deposited my bag and went outside. I couldn't see him anywhere. I went back inside.

"Anybody seen Vern yet?"

I addressed my question as casually as possible to my tent-mates, a vague anxiety gripping my heart. No, they said, they hadn't seen Vern anywhere. I went back outside. Coming up the street toward me I saw Bill Atkinson and my brother Jack and a third person between them, a boy named Kennedy. I knew what was going to happen. I dived back into the tent, picked up my stave, and came out to face them.

"He's not coming in here," I said, pointing the tip of my stave at Kennedy. "Where's Vern?"

"Vern's going to be in another tent," Atkinson said.

"You fucking bastards!" I shouted. "You moved him to another tent on purpose."

And I ducked in through the flap and started laying about me. I whacked duffel bags, cots, the centre pole, the canvas walls, the other boys too, their shin bones and arses as they fled through the flap of the tent, yelling that Luke had gone

35

berserk. Atkinson and Jack came inside and circled me cautiously. I knew I was done for, and when I made a half-hearted swing Atkinson caught the stave with his hand while Jack grabbed me and pinned my arms.

Atkinson leaned down and took me by the shoulders, looking into my face. "Listen now Luke! It was Vern himself who asked to be moved to another tent."

"I don't believe you," I said. "You put him over with Gary Greeley, didn't you?"

"What difference does it make?" Jack said impatiently. "He's gone and you just got to accept it. Grow up, for Christ's sake!"

And I knew it was true. Vern was over with Gary Greeley. I had been betrayed.

Jack had let go of my arms when Atkinson took my shoulders and I spun now and hit him in the stomach with all my might. He made an *oufff* sound and grabbed my arms again.

"You stubborn little bugger!" he said, and then to Atkinson, "I'd better take him with me to my tent."

I sulked for the next ten days, a malicious sulk. I watched Vern and Gary from a distance, happy in their horseplay together—and their jerking off, I was sure—but I stayed away from them, Jack always at my shoulder in case I tried to start anything, like a fight. On our tours of the city, in restaurants and in stores, on the streets, people made a big deal over us boys with Newfoundland on our shoulder patches. We were something new, real curiosities, and again, as with the scouts from other provinces, I felt there was something odd in the way they petted us. I was in no mood for petting and stroking. I hated the people, shrugging them off, sometimes cursing deliberately to shock them. I hated the city. The monuments, the Parliament buildings, the museums, all of it barely registered on my consciousness. Once, on a visit to the Peace Tower, I got my hands on Jack's Box Brownie on the pretense of taking a picture I'd promised our mother and then dropped it from the top. I watched the little black box fall all the way down, watched it break apart into a hundred pieces on the stone below, exposing the film. The reason? That

36

morning, on the same roll of film that was in the camera that I dropped, Jack had taken a picture of the boys from the 3rd St. John's on Parliament Hill with Mounties posed on either side and in *my* place next to Vern—who was always kneeling in the centre of the front row in every picture, school, sports, whatever—there crouched a grinning Gary Greeley.

"It slipped from my hands," I said to Jack, "I couldn't help it."

The shows were put on every evening. At dusk, all the scouts and visitors from the city would gather at a field adjacent to the campsite. A large grandstand on one side of the field was for the visitors; the scouts from all the Provinces except the one putting on the show sat on the ground along the two sides of the field at right angles to the grandstand; the fourth side opposite the grandstand had a canvas fence like a curtain through which the scouts from the Province putting on the show would emerge. Newfoundland's turn was on the last night. Nova Scotia had done highland games and dancing; Alberta had staged a chuckwagon race without horses, the boys towing the wagons; the Ontario crowd had run onto the field with each pair of boys carrying a log, and then they'd put them all together to make a huge construction—something like Vern's and my Meccano creations—building it up higher and higher and finally planting the Canadian flag on the top, the boys clinging all over the thing, saluting.

Well, they hadn't seen anything yet!

"Now then b'ys!" Uncle Louis exhorted us behind the canvas fence, "Let's show them what we're made of! March like heroes and bawl your lungs out when we comes to the 'Rant 'n Roar!'"

And with "Colonel Bogie" blaring over the public address system and Uncle Louis strutting stiffly out front, we swung onto the field like a Guards regiment, our staves-for-rifles held rigidly straight up and down at our left sides, our right arms swinging up parallel to the ground. We had come out in column formation and I don't know what the audience thought we were doing, but there was a lot of cheering. We broke neatly out into line abreast, came to a perfect foot-stomping halt, and bellowed out our old national anthem:

> *As loved our fathers so we love,*
> *Where once they stood we stand,*
> *Our prayers we raise to heaven above,*
> *God guard thee, Newfoundland!*
> *God guard thee! God guard thee!*
> *God guard thee Newfoundland!*

More cheers and applause, and off around the field we marched. Slow march, double time, reform column, space out the ranks, stop and sing. When we used to do "Lukey's Boat" in rehearsal I'd put on goofy faces and bring out smiles all around, but I'd been such a dark presence for the last ten days I don't think anyone was expecting anything from me anymore, and they didn't get it. I was surprised they'd even let me march for fear I'd do something deliberate to screw up our show, like stick my stave between Gary Greeley's feet. But I had a good voice and they needed me for the solo part in "Let Me Fish Off Cape St. Mary's." I liked performing and I sang creditably well, still hoping for Vern's eyes on me all the while. *What won't you do, Luke?* When I finished and Uncle Louis pointed me out, I stepped forward and took my bow without any foolishness. We marched some more, sang the obligatory "Squid Jigging Grounds," bawled our way through "We'll Rant and We'll Roar Like True Newfoundlanders," and then brought down the house when we stood rigidly at attention and ended with "Oh Canada!" The next morning, when Vern and Gary were over in the showers, I slipped into their tent and stole their sealskin hat-bands and sold them for cash, ten bucks apiece.

The rest of that summer was the most miserable time of my life. To add insult to injury, when we got back home Gary Greeley stole my girlfriend, and he and Nancy and Vern and Shirley double dated and went off to Mount Pearl together where, I heard, they did "things" in the woods—Nancy had told somebody who told somebody who told me that all *I* ever did was talk and talk. I refused to ride my girl's bike anymore, so I walked the streets to the evening ball games alone, took the bus to the Bowring Park swimming-pool alone, all the time feeling very sorry for myself. And all the while in bed at night I kept trying, complaining afterwards to Jack that it was never going to happen. "Keep at it kid," he said, "it'll come." Eventually, one night in early October, "it" did come. With a cry of surprise, my first orgasm dawned in me like the sun rising on a new world. I soon forgot about Vern Tibbo— *How are the mighty fallen!* And I soon forgot, too, that from the train leaving Ottawa I had looked back across the river at the Peace Tower and vowed that I would remember this moment forever, like people do sometimes when leaving a place where they have been happy, except that for me Ottawa had been a place that I'd hated, and that during the long tail-end of summer my hatred had escalated to include all that the city stood for: if we hadn't gone to Ottawa, I reasoned, I wouldn't be so unhappy; and if there hadn't been a Jamboree we wouldn't have gone to Ottawa; and if there hadn't been any Confederation with Canada there wouldn't have been any Jamboree. And so, for a few lonely months that year, I was my father's true disciple—I blamed Canada for everything.

39

Family Furnishings

Alice Munro

Alfrida. My father called her Freddie. The two of them were
first cousins and lived for a while on adjoining farms. One
day, they were out in the fields of stubble playing with my
father's dog, whose name was Mack. The sun was shining but
did not melt the ice in the furrows. They stomped on the ice
and enjoyed its crackle underfoot.

"How could you remember a thing like that?" my father said.
"You made it up."
   "I did not."
   "You did so."
   "I did not."

All of a sudden, they heard bells pealing, whistles blowing.
The town bell and the church bells were ringing. The factory
whistles were blowing, in the town three miles away. The
world had burst its seams for joy, and Mack tore out to the
road, because he was sure a parade was coming. It was the end
of the First World War.

Three times a week, we could read Alfrida's name in the
paper. Just her first name—Alfrida. It was printed as if written by hand, a flowing fountain-pen signature. Round and
About the Town, with Alfrida. The town mentioned was not
the one close by but the city to the south, where Alfrida lived,
and which my family visited perhaps once every two or three
years.

Now is the time for all you future June brides to start registering your preferences at the China Cabinet, and I must tell you that if I were a bride-to-be—which, alas, I am not—I might resist all the patterned dinner sets, exquisite as they are, and go for the pearly-white, the ultra-modern Rosenthal....

Beauty treatments may come and beauty treatments may go, but the masks they slather on you at Fantine's Salon are guaranteed—speaking of brides—to make your skin bloom like orange blossoms. And to make the bride's mom, and the bride's aunts and, for all I know, her grandmom, feel as if they had just taken a dip in the Fountain of Youth.

You would never have expected Alfrida to write in this style, from the way she talked. She was also one of the people who wrote under the name of Flora Simpson on the Flora Simpson Housewives' Page. Women from all over the countryside believed that they were writing their letters to the plump woman with crimped grey hair and a forgiving smile who was pictured at the top of the page. But the truth—which I was not to tell—was that the notes responding to each of the letters were produced by Alfrida and a man she called Horse Henry, who also did the obituaries. The women who wrote in gave themselves such names as Morning Star and Lily of the Valley and Little Annie Rooney and Dishmop Queen. Some names were so popular that numbers had to be assigned to them—Goldilocks 1, Goldilocks 2, Goldilocks 3.

"Dear Morning Star," Alfrida or Horse Henry would write. "Eczema is a dreadful pest, especially in this hot weather we're having, and I hope that the baking soda does some good. Home treatments certainly ought to be respected, but it never hurts to seek out your doctor's advice. It's splendid to hear that your hubby is up and about again. It can't have been any fun with *both* of you under the weather."

In all the small towns of that part of Ontario, housewives who belonged to the Flora Simpson Club would hold an annual summer picnic. Flora Simpson always sent her special greetings but explained that there were just too many events for her to show up at all of them, and she did not like to make distinctions. Alfrida said that there had been talk of sending Horse Henry done up in a wig and pillow bosoms, or even Alfrida herself leering like the witch of Babylon (not even she, at my parents' table, would quote the Bible accurately and say "whore") with a ciggie-boo stuck to her lipstick. "But, oh," she said, "the paper would kill us. And anyway it would be too mean."

She always called her cigarettes "ciggie-boos." When I was fifteen or sixteen, she leaned across the table and asked, "How would you like a ciggie-boo, too?" The meal was finished, and my father had started to roll his own. He shook his head.

I said thank you and let Alfrida light me a cigarette and smoked for the first time in front of my parents. They pretended that it was a great joke.

"Ah, will you look at your daughter?" my mother said to my father. She rolled her eyes and clapped her hands to her chest and spoke in an artificial, languishing voice. "I'm like to faint."

"Have to get the horsewhip out," my father said, half rising in his chair.

This moment was amazing. It was as if Alfrida had transformed us into new people. Ordinarily, my mother would have said that she didn't like to see a woman smoke. And when she said in a certain tone that she didn't like something, it was as if she were drawing on a private source of wisdom, which was unassailable and almost sacred. It was when she reached for this tone, and the expression of listening to inner voices that accompanied it, that I particularly hated her.

As for my father, he had beaten me, in that very room, not with a horsewhip but with his belt, for running afoul of my mother's rules and wounding her feelings. Now it seemed that such beatings could occur only in another universe.

My parents had been put in a corner by Alfrida—and also by me—but they had responded so gamely and gracefully that it was really as if all three of us, my mother and my father and myself, had been lifted to a new level of ease and aplomb. In that instant, I could see them—particularly my mother—as being capable of a kind of lightheartedness that was hardly

42

ever on view.

All thanks to Alfrida.

In my family, Alfrida was always referred to as a "career girl." This made her seem younger than my parents, though she was about the same age. She was also said to be a city person. And "the city," when it was spoken of in this way, meant the one where she lived and worked. But it meant something else as well. It was not just a distinct configuration of buildings and sidewalks and streetcar lines, or even a crowding together of people; it was something more abstract, something like a hive of bees—stormy but organized, sometimes dangerous. Most people went into such a place only when they had to and were glad when they got out. Some, however, were attracted to it—as Alfrida must have been, long ago, and as I was now, puffing on my cigarette and trying to hold it in a nonchalant way, although it seemed to have grown to the size of a baseball bat between my fingers.

My family did not have a regular social life—friends did not come to the house for dinner, let alone for parties. It was a matter of class, maybe. The parents of the boy I married—about five years after this scene at the dinner table—invited people who were not related to them to dinner, and they went to afternoon parties, which they spoke of, unselfconsciously, as cocktail parties. Theirs was a life I had read of in magazines, and it seemed to me to place my in-laws in a world of storybook privilege.

What our family did was put boards in the dining-room table two or three times a year, in order to entertain my grandmother and my aunts—my father's two older sisters—and their husbands. We did this at Christmas or at Thanksgiving, when it was our turn, and perhaps also when a relative from another part of the province showed up on a visit.

My mother and I would start preparing for such dinners a couple of days ahead. We ironed the good tablecloth, which was as heavy as a bed quilt, and washed the good dishes, which had been sitting in the china cabinet collecting dust, and wiped down the legs of the dining-room chairs, as well as making the jellied salads, the pies and cakes, that had to accompany the roast turkey or baked ham and bowls of vegetables. There had to be far too much to eat, and most of the conversation at the table concerned the food, with the company saying how good it was and being urged to have more, and saying that they couldn't, they were stuffed, and then relenting, taking just a little more, and saying that they shouldn't, they were ready to bust. And dessert still to come.

There was hardly any idea of general conversation, and in fact there was a feeling that conversation that passed beyond certain limits might be a disruption, a form of showing off. My mother's understanding of the limits was not reliable, and she sometimes couldn't wait out the pauses or honour the common aversion to follow-up. So when somebody said, "Seen Harley upstreet yesterday. Harley Cook," she was liable to say, perhaps, "Do you think a man like Harley is a confirmed bachelor? Or he just hasn't met the right person?" As if, when you mentioned seeing Harley Cook, you were bound to have something further to say about him, something *interesting*.

Then there might be a silence, not because the people at the table meant to be rude but because they were flummoxed. Until my father said, with embarrassment and oblique reproach, "He seems to get on all right by hisself."(If his family had not been present, he would more likely have said "himself.")

And everybody else went on cutting, spooning, swallowing, in the glare of the fresh tablecloth and the bright light pouring in through the newly washed windows. These dinners were always in the middle of the day.

The people at that table were quite capable of talk. Washing and drying the dishes in the kitchen, the aunts would talk about who had a tumour, a septic throat, a bad mess of boils. They would tell how their own digestions, kidneys, nerves were functioning. Intimate bodily matters never seemed to be so out of place, or suspect, as the mention of a fact read in a magazine, or an item in the news, or anything, really, that was not material close at hand. Meanwhile, resting on the porch, or during a brief walk out to look at the crops, the aunts' husbands would pass on the information that somebody was in a tight spot with the bank, or still owed money on an expensive piece of machinery, or had invested in a bull that was a disappointment on the job.

It could have been that they felt clamped down by the formality of our dining-room, the presence of bread-and-butter plates and dessert spoons, when it was the custom to put a piece of pie right onto a dinner plate that had been cleaned up with bread. (It would have been an offence, however, for us not to set things out in this proper way, and in their own houses, on like occasions, they would put their guests through the same paces.) It may have been just that eating was one thing, and talking was something else.

When Alfrida came it was another story altogether. The good cloth would be spread and the good dishes would be out. My mother would have gone to a lot of trouble with the food, and she'd be nervous about the results—probably she would have abandoned the usual turkey and stuffing and mashed potatoes and made something like chicken salad surrounded by mounds of moulded rice with cut-up pimentos, and this would be followed by a dessert involving gelatin and egg whites and whipped cream which took a long, nerve-racking time to set because we had no refrigerator and it had to be chilled on the cellar floor. But the constraint, the required pall over the table, was quite absent. Alfrida not only accepted second helpings, she asked for them. And she did this almost absent-mindedly, tossing off her compliments in the same way, as if the food, the eating of the food, were a secondary though agreeable thing, and she were really there to talk, and make other people talk, and anything you wanted to talk about—almost anything—would be fine.

She always visited in summer, and usually she wore some sort of striped, silky sundress, with a halter top that left her back bare. Her back was not pretty, being sprinkled with little dark moles, and her shoulders were bony and her chest was nearly flat. My father would always remark on how much she could eat and remain thin. (One thing that was not considered out of place in our family was direct comment, to somebody's face, about fatness or skinniness or pallor or ruddiness or baldness.)

Alfrida's dark hair was done up in rolls above her face and at the sides, in the style of the time. Her skin was freckled and netted with fine wrinkles, and her mouth wide, the lower lip rather thick, almost drooping, painted with a hearty lipstick that left a smear on her teacup and water tumbler. When her mouth was opened wide—as it nearly always was, talking or laughing—you could see that some of her teeth had been pulled, at the back. Nobody would have said that she was good-looking—any woman over 25 seemed to me to have pretty well passed beyond the possibility of being good-looking, or, at least, to have lost the right to be so, and perhaps even the desire—but she was fervent and dashing and she lit up a room.

Alfrida talked to my father about things that were happening in the world, about politics. My father read the paper, he listened to the radio, and he had opinions about these things but rarely got a chance to talk about them. The aunts' husbands had opinions, too, but theirs were brief and unvaried and expressed an everlasting distrust of all public figures and particularly all foreigners, so that most of the time all that could be got out of them were grunts of dismissal. My grandmother was deaf—nobody could tell how much she knew or what she thought about anything—and the aunts themselves seemed fairly proud of how much they didn't know or didn't have to pay attention to. My mother had been a schoolteacher, and she could readily have pointed out all the countries of Europe on the map, but she saw the world through a personal haze, with the British Empire and the Royal Family looming large, and everything else diminished, thrown into a jumble heap that was easy for her to disregard.

Alfrida's views were not really so far removed from the uncles'. Or so it appeared. But, instead of grunting and letting the subject go, she gave her hooting laugh, and told stories about prime ministers and the American President and John L. Lewis and the Mayor of Montreal—stories in which they all came out badly. She told stories about the Royal Family, too, but there she made a distinction between the good ones, like the King and Queen and the beautiful Duchess of Kent, and the dreadful ones, like the Windsors and old King Eddy, who, she implied, had a certain disease and had marked his wife's neck by trying to strangle her, which was why she always had to wear her pearls. This distinction coincided pretty well with one my mother made but seldom spoke of, so she did not object—though the reference to syphilis made her wince.

I smiled at it, knowingly, and with a foolhardy composure.

Alfrida called the Russians funny names. Mikoyan-sky. Uncle Joe-sky. She believed that they were pulling the wool over everybody's eyes, and that the United Nations was a farce that would never work and that Japan would rise again and should have been finished off when there was the chance. She didn't trust Quebec, either. Or the Pope, whom she called "the Poop." And there was a problem for her with Senator McCarthy—she would have liked to be on his side, but his being a Catholic was a stumbling block.

Sometimes it seemed as if she were putting on a show—a display, maybe, to tease my father. To rile him up, as he himself would have said, to get his goat. But not because she disliked him or even wanted to make him uncomfortable. Quite the opposite. She seemed to be tormenting him almost as young girls torment boys at school, where arguments are a peculiar delight to both sides and insults are taken as flattery. My father argued with her always in a mild steady voice, and yet it was clear that he, too, had the intention of goading her on. Sometimes he would do a turnaround, and say that maybe she was right—that with her work on the newspaper, she must have sources of information that he didn't have. "You've put me straight," he'd say. "If I had any sense, I'd be obliged to you." And she'd say, "Don't give me that load of baloney."

"You two," my mother said, in mock despair and perhaps in real exhaustion, and Alfrida told her to go and have a lie-down—she deserved it after this splendiferous dinner, and Alfrida and I would manage the dishes. My mother was subject to a tremor in her right arm, a stiffness in her fingers, that she believed came when she got overtired.

While we worked in the kitchen, Alfrida talked to me about celebrities—actors, even minor movie stars, who had made stage appearances in the city where she lived. In a low-ered voice broken by wildly disrespectful laughter, she told me rumours about their bad behaviour, the private scandals that had never made it into the magazines. She mentioned

47

queers, artificial bosoms, household triangles—all things I had found hints of in my reading but felt giddy to hear about, even at third or fourth hand, in real life.

Alfrida's teeth always got my attention, so that, even during these confidential recitals, I sometimes lost track of what was being said. Her front teeth were all of a slightly different colour, no two alike. Some tended toward shades of dark ivory; others were opalescent, shadowed with lilac, and gave out fish-flashes of silver rims, occasionally a gleam of gold. People's teeth then seldom made such a solid, handsome show as they do now—unless they were false—but Alfrida's were unusual in their individuality, clear separation, and size. When Alfrida let out some jibe that was especially, knowingly outrageous, they seemed to leap to the fore like jolly spear fighters.

"She always did have trouble with her teeth," the aunts said. "She had that abscess, remember—the poison went all through her body."

How like them, I thought, to pick on any weakness in a superior person, to zoom in on any physical distress.

"Why doesn't she just have them all out and be done with it?" they said.

"Likely she couldn't afford it," my grandmother said, surprising everybody, as she sometimes did, by showing that she had been keeping up with a conversation all along.

And surprising me with the new, everyday sort of light this shone on Alfrida's life. I had believed that Alfrida was rich, at least in comparison with the rest of the family. She lived in an apartment—I had never seen it, but to me that fact conveyed at least the idea of a very civilized life—and she wore clothes that were not homemade, and her shoes were not Oxfords like the shoes of practically all the other grownup women I knew; they were sandals made of bright strips of plastic. It was hard to know whether my grandmother was simply living in the past, when getting your teeth done was the solemn, crowning expense of a lifetime, or whether she really knew things about Alfrida's life that I would not have guessed.

The rest of the family was never present when Alfrida had dinner at our house. She did go to see my grandmother, who was her aunt, her mother's sister, and who lived alternately

48

with one or the other of my aunts. Alfrida went to whichever house my grandmother was staying in at the time, but the meal she took was always with us. Usually she came to our house first and visited awhile, and then gathered herself up, as if reluctantly, to make the other visit. When she came back later and we sat down to eat, nothing derogatory was said outright, against the aunts and their husbands, and certainly nothing disrespectful about my grandmother. In fact, it was the way that Alfrida spoke of my grandmother—with a sudden sobriety and concern in her voice (what about her blood pressure, had she been to the doctor lately?)—that made me aware of the difference, of the coolness or restraint with which she asked after the others. There would be a similar restraint in my mother's reply, and an extra gravity in my father's—almost a caricature of gravity—that showed how they all agreed about something they could not say.

On the day I smoked the cigarette, Alfrida decided to take this routine a bit further, and she said somberly, "How about Asa then? Is he still as much of a conversation-grabber as ever?"

My father shook his head sadly, as if the thought of his brother-in-law's garrulousness must weigh us all down.

"Indeed," he said. "He is indeed."

Then I took my chance.

"Looks like the roundworms have got into the hogs," I said. "Yup."

Except for the "yup," this was just what my uncle had recently said, and he had said it at this very table, being overcome by an uncharacteristic need to break the silence or to pass on something important that had just come to mind. And I said it with just his stately grunts, his innocent solemnity.

Alfrida gave a great approving laugh, showing her festive teeth.

My father bent over his plate, as if to hide how he was laughing, too, but of course not really hiding it, and mother shook her head, biting her lips together, smiling. I felt a keen triumph. Nothing was said to put me in my place, no reproof for what was sometimes called my "sarcasm," my "being

49

smart." The word "smart," when it was used about me, in the family, might mean intelligent, in which case it was used rather grudgingly—"oh, she's smart enough some ways"—or it might be used to mean pushy, attention-seeking, obnoxious. *Don't be so smart.*

Sometimes my mother said, "You have a cruel tongue."

Sometimes—this was a great deal worse—my father was disgusted with me. "What makes you think you have the right to run down decent people?"

This day nothing like that happened. I seemed to be as free as a visitor at the table, almost as free as Alfrida, and flourishing under the banner of my own personality.

But a gap was about to open, and perhaps that was the last time, the very last time, that Alfrida sat at our table. Christmas cards continued to be exchanged, possibly even letters—as long as my mother could manage a pen—and we still saw Alfrida's name in the paper, but I cannot recall any visits during the last couple of years I lived at home.

It may have been that Alfrida had asked if she could bring her friend, and been told that she could not. If she was already living with him, that would have been one reason, and, if he was the same man she lived with later, the fact that he was married would have been another. My parents would have been united in this. My mother had a horror of irregular sex or flaunted sex—of any sex, you might say, for the proper, married kind was not acknowledged at all—and my father, too, judged these matters strictly, at that time in his life. He might have had a special objection, also, to any man who could get a hold over Alfrida. She would have made herself cheap, in my parents' eyes.

But she may not have asked at all; she may have known enough not to. During the time of those lively visits there may have been no man in her life, and then, when there was one, her attention may have shifted entirely.

Or she may have been wary of the special atmosphere of a household where there is a sick person who will go on getting sicker and never get better. Which was the case with my mother, whose odd symptoms joined together, and turned a corner, and instead of an inconvenience became her whole destiny.

"The poor thing," the aunts said.

And as my mother was changed from a mother into a stricken presence around the house, the other, formerly so restricted, females in the family seemed to gain some little liveliness and increased competence in the world. My grandmother got herself a hearing aid—something nobody would have suggested to her. One of the aunts' husbands—not Asa, but the one named Irvine—died, and the aunt who had been married to him learned to drive a car and got a job doing alterations in a clothing store and no longer wore a hairnet.

They called in to see my mother, and always saw the same thing—that the one who had been better looking, who had never quite let them forget that she was a schoolteacher, was growing month by month slower and stiffer in the movements of her limbs and thicker and more importunate in her speech, and that nothing was going to help her.

They told me to take good care of her. "She's your mother," they reminded me. "The poor thing."

Alfrida would not have been able to say those things, and she might not have been able to find anything to say in their place. Her not coming to see us was all right with me. I didn't want people coming. I had no time for them. I had become a furious housekeeper, waxing the floors and ironing even the dish-towels, and it was all done to keep some sort of disgrace (my mother's deterioration seemed to be a unique disgrace that infected us all) at bay. It was done to make it seem as if I lived in a normal family in an ordinary house, but the moment somebody stepped in our door and saw my mother they saw that this was not so and they pitied us. A thing I could not stand.

I won a scholarship, and I didn't stay home to take care of my mother or of anything else. The college I went to was in the city where Alfrida lived. After a few months, she invited me to supper, but I couldn't go, because I worked every evening of the week except Sundays—in the city library, downtown, and in the college library, both of which stayed open until nine o'clock. Sometime later, during the winter, Alfrida asked me again, and this time the invitation was for a Sunday. I told her that I couldn't come because I was going to a concert.

"Oh—a date?" she said, and I said yes, but at the time it wasn't true. I would go to the free Sunday concerts in the college auditorium, with another girl, or two or three other girls, for something to do and in the faint hope of meeting some boys.

"Well, you'll have to bring him around sometime," Alfrida said. "I'm dying to meet him."

Toward the end of the year I did have someone to bring, and I had actually met him at a concert. But I would never have brought him to meet Alfrida. I would never have brought any of my new friends to meet her. My new friends were people who said, "Have you read *Look Homeward, Angel*? Oh, you have to read that. Have you read *Buddenbrooks*?" They were people with whom I went to see "Forbidden Games" and "Les Enfants du Paradis," when the Film Society brought them in. The boy I went out with, and later became engaged to, had taken me to the Music Building, where you could listen to records at lunch hour. He introduced me to Gounod, and because of Gounod I loved opera, and because of opera I loved Mozart.

When Alfrida left a message at my rooming-house, asking me to call back, I never did. After that, she didn't call again.

She still wrote for the paper. Occasionally I glanced at one of her rhapsodies about Royal Doulton figurines or imported ginger biscuits or honeymoon negligees. But now that I was living in the city, I seldom looked at the paper that had once seemed to me to be the centre of its life—and even, in a way, the centre of our life at home, 60 miles away. The jokes, the compulsive insincerity, of people like Alfrida and Horse Henry now struck me as tawdry and boring.

I did not worry about running into her, even in this city that was not, after all, so very large. I never went into the shops that she mentioned in her column, and she lived far away from my rooming-house, somewhere on the south side of town.

Nor did I think that Alfrida was the kind of person to show

up at the library. The very word "library" would probably make her turn down her big mouth in a parody of consternation, as she used to do at the books in the bookcase in our house—some of them won as school prizes by my teenage parents (there was my mother's maiden name, in her beautiful, lost handwriting), books that seemed to me not like things bought in a store at all but like presences in the house, just as the trees outside the window were not plants but presences rooted in the ground. *The Mill on the Floss, The Call of the Wild, The Heart of Midlothian.* "Lot of hot-shot reading in there," Alfrida had said. "Bet you don't crack those very often." And my father had said no, he didn't, falling in with her comradely tone of dismissal, and to some extent telling a lie, because he did look into them, once in a long while, when he had the time.

That was the kind of lie I hoped never to have to tell, about the things that really mattered to me. And in order not to, I would pretty well have to stay clear of the people I used to know.

At the end of my second year, I was leaving college—my scholarship had covered only two years there. But it didn't matter. I was planning to be a writer, anyway. And I was getting married.

Alfrida had got word of this, and she got in touch with me again.

"I guess you must've been too busy to call me, or maybe nobody ever gave you my messages," she said.

I said that maybe I had been, or maybe they hadn't.

This time I agreed to visit. A visit would not commit me to anything, since I was not going to be living in this city in the future. I picked a Sunday, in the middle of May, just after my final exams were over, when my fiancé was going to be in Ottawa for a job interview. The day was bright and sunny, and I decided to walk. There were parts of the city that were still entirely strange to me. The shade trees along the northern street had just come out in leaf, and the lilacs, the ornamental crabapple trees, and the beds of tulips were all in flower, the lawns like fresh carpets. But, after a while, I found myself walking along streets where there were no shade trees, streets where the houses were hardly an arm's reach from the sidewalk, and where such lilacs as there were—lilacs will grow anywhere—were pale, as if sun-bleached, and their fragrance did not carry. On these streets, in addition to the houses, there were narrow apartment buildings, only two or three storeys high, some with the utilitarian decoration of a rim of glass bricks around their doors, and some with raised windows and limp curtains falling out over their sills.

Alfrida's apartment was the whole upstairs of a house. The downstairs—at least the front part of the downstairs—had been turned into a shop, which was closed, it being Sunday. It was a secondhand shop—I could see through the dirty front windows a lot of nondescript furniture with stacks of old dishes and utensils set everywhere. The only thing that caught my eye was a honey pail, exactly like the honey pail with a blue sky and a golden beehive in which I had carried my lunch to school when I was six or seven years old. I could remember reading over and over the words on its side: "All pure honey will granulate."

I had no idea what "granulate" meant, but I liked the sound of it—it seemed ornate and delicious.

I had taken longer to get there than I had expected, and I was very hot. I had not thought that Alfrida, inviting me to lunch, would present me with a meal like the Sunday dinners at home, but it was cooked chicken and vegetables I smelled as I climbed the outdoor stairway.

"I thought you'd got lost," Alfrida called out above me. "I was about to get up a rescue party."

Instead of a sundress, she was wearing a pink blouse with a floppy bow at the neck, tucked into a pleated brown skirt. Her hair was no longer done up in smooth rolls but cut short and frizzed around her face, its dark brown now harshly touched with red. And her face, which I remembered as lean and summer-tanned, had got fuller and somewhat pouchy. In the noon light, her makeup stood out on her skin like orange-pink paint.

But the biggest difference was that she had got false teeth, of a uniform colour, slightly overfilling her mouth and giving

54

an anxious edge to her old expression of slapdash eagerness.

"Well—haven't you plumped out," she said. "You used to be so skinny."

This was true, but I did not like to hear it. Along with all the girls at the rooming-house, I ate cheap food—copious meals of Kraft Dinner and packages of jam-filled cookies. My fiancé, so sturdily and possessively in favour of everything about me, said that he liked full-bodied women and that I reminded him of Jane Russell. I did not mind his saying that, but I was affronted when other people had anything to say about my appearance. Particularly when it was somebody like Alfrida, somebody who had lost all importance in my life. I really believed that such people had no right to be looking at me, or forming any opinions about me, let alone stating them.

The house was narrow across the front but long from front to back. There was a living-room, whose ceilings sloped at the sides and whose windows overlooked the street, a hall-like dining-room with no windows at all, a kitchen, a bathroom also without windows that got its daylight through a pebbled-glass pane in the door, and, across the back of the house, a glassed-in sunporch.

The sloping ceilings made the rooms look makeshift, as if they were only pretending to be anything but bedrooms. But they were crowded with serious furniture—dining-room table and chairs, kitchen table and chairs, living-room sofa and recliner—all meant for larger, proper rooms. Doilies on the tables, squares of embroidered white cloth protecting the backs and arms of the sofa and chairs, sheer curtains across the windows and heavy flowered curtains at the sides—it was all more like the aunts' houses than I would have thought possible. And on the dining-room wall—not in the bathroom or the bedroom but in the dining-room—there hung a picture that was a silhouette of a girl in a hoopskirt, all constructed of pink satin ribbon.

Alfrida seemed to guess something of what I was thinking.

"I know I've got far too much stuff in here," she said. "But it's my parents' stuff. It's family furnishings, and I couldn't let it go."

I had never thought of her as having parents. As far as I

55

knew, Alfrida's mother had died when she was six years old, and she had been brought up by my grandmother, who was her aunt.

"My dad and mother's," Alfrida said. "When Dad went off, your grandma stored it all in her back room and the basement and the shed, because she thought it ought to be mine when I grew up, and so here it is. I couldn't turn it down, when she went to that trouble."

Now it came back to me—the part of Alfrida's life that I had forgotten about. Alfrida's father had married again. He had left the farm and got a job working for the railway. He had had some other children, and sometimes Alfrida used to mention them, in a joking way that had something to do with how many children there had been and how quickly they had followed one another.

"Come and meet Bill," Alfrida said.

Bill was out on the sunporch. He sat as if waiting to be summoned, on a low couch or daybed that was covered with a brown plaid blanket. The blanket was rumpled—he must have been lying on it recently—and the blinds on the windows were pulled down to their sills. The light in the room— the hot sunlight coming through rain-marked yellow blinds —and the rough blanket and faded, dented cushion, even the smell of the blanket and of the masculine slippers, old, scuffed slippers that had lost their shape and pattern, reminded me, just as much as the doilies and the heavy, polished furniture in the inner rooms had done, of my aunts' houses. There, too, you could come upon a shabby male hideaway with its furtive yet insistent odours, its shamefaced but stubborn rejection of the female domain.

Bill stood up and shook my hand, however, as the uncles would never have done with a strange girl. Or with any girl. No specific rudeness would have held them back—just a dread of appearing ceremonious.

He was a tall man with wavy, glistening grey hair and a smooth but not youthful face. A handsome man, with the force of his good looks somehow drained away by indifferent health or bad luck or lack of gumption. But he still had a worn courtesy, a way of bending toward a woman, which suggested that the meeting would be a pleasure, for her and for himself.

Alfrida directed us into the windowless dining-room, where the lights were on in the middle of this bright day. I got the impression that the meal had been ready some time ago, and that my late arrival had delayed their usual schedule. Bill served the roast chicken and dressing, Alfrida the vegetables. Alfrida said to Bill, "Honey, what do you think that is beside your plate?" and then he remembered to pick up his napkin.

He did not have much to say. He offered the gravy; he inquired as to whether I wanted mustard relish or salt and pepper; he followed the conversation by turning his head toward Alfrida or toward me. Every so often he made a little whistling sound between his teeth, a shivery sound that seemed meant to be genial and appreciative and that I thought at first might be a prelude to some remark. But it never was, and Alfrida never paused for it. I have since seen reformed drinkers who behaved somewhat as he did—chiming in agreeably but unable to carry things beyond that, helplessly preoccupied. I never knew whether Bill was one of them, but he did seem to carry around a history of defeat, of troubles borne and lessons learned, and he had an air, too, of gallant accommodation for whatever choices had gone wrong or chances hadn't panned out.

These were frozen peas and carrots, Alfrida said. Frozen vegetables were fairly new at the time.

"They beat the canned," she said. "They're practically as good as fresh."

Then Bill made a whole statement. He said that they were better than fresh. The colour, the flavour, everything was better than fresh. He said that it was remarkable what they could do now and what would be done by way of freezing things in the future.

Alfrida leaned forward, smiling. She seemed almost to hold her breath, as if he were her child taking unsupported steps, or a first lone wobble on a bicycle.

There was a way they could inject something into a chicken, he told us, a new process that would have every chicken coming out the same—plump and tasty. No such thing as taking a risk on getting an inferior chicken anymore.

"Bill's field is chemistry," Alfrida said.

When I had nothing to say to this, she added, "He worked for Gooderhams."

Still nothing.

"The distillers," she said. "Gooderhams whiskey."

The reason that I had nothing to say was not that I was rude or bored (or any more rude than I was naturally at that time, or more bored than I had expected to be) but that I did not understand that I should ask questions—almost any questions at all, to draw a shy male into conversation, to shake him out of his abstraction, and set him up as a man of a certain authority, and therefore the man of the house. I did not understand why Alfrida looked at him with such a fiercely encouraging smile. All my experience of women with men— of a woman listening to her man and hoping that he will establish himself as somebody that she can reasonably be proud of—was in the future. The only observation that I had made of couples was of my aunts and uncles and of my mother and father, and those husbands and wives seemed to have remote and formalized connections and no obvious dependence on each other.

Bill continued eating as if he had not heard this mention of his profession and his employer, and Alfrida began to question me about my courses. She was still smiling, but her smile had changed. There was a little twitch of impatience and unpleasantness in it, as if she were just waiting for me to get to the end of my explanations so that she could say—as she did say—"You couldn't get me to read that stuff for a million dollars."

"Life's too short," she went on. "You know, down at the paper we sometimes get somebody that's been through all that. Honours English. Honours Philosophy. You don't know what to do with them. They can't write worth a nickel. I've told you that, haven't I?" she said to Bill, and Bill looked up and gave her his dutiful smile.

"So what do you do for fun?" Alfrida said, sometime later.

"A Streetcar Named Desire" was playing at a theatre in Toronto at that time, and I told her that I had gone down on the train with a couple of friends to see it.

Alfrida let her knife and fork clatter onto her plate.

"That filth!" she cried. Her face leapt out at me, carved with sudden anger and disgust. Then she spoke more calmly but still with a virulent displeasure.

"You went all the way to Toronto to see that filth."

We had finished the dessert, and Bill picked that moment to ask if he might be excused. He asked Alfrida, then with the slightest bow he asked me. He went back to the sunporch and in a little while we could smell his pipe. Alfrida, watching him go, seemed to forget about me and the play. There was a look of such stricken tenderness on her face that, when she stood up, I thought she was going to follow him. But she was only going to get her cigarettes.

She held them out to me and, when I took one, she said, with a deliberate effort at jollity, "I see you kept up the bad habit I got you started on." It seemed as if she had remembered that I was not a child anymore and that I did not have to be in her house and there was no point in making an enemy of me. And I wasn't going to argue—I did not care what Alfrida thought about Tennessee Williams. Or what she thought about anything else.

"I guess it's your own business," Alfrida said. "You can go where you want to go." And she added, "After all—you'll be a married woman pretty soon."

By her tone, this could have meant, "I have to allow that you're grownup now," or "Pretty soon you'll have to toe the line."

We got up and started to collect the dishes. Working close to each other in the small space between the kitchen table and counter and the refrigerator, we soon developed, without speaking about it, a certain order and harmony of scraping and stacking and putting the leftover food into smaller containers for storage and filling the sink with hot, soapy water. We brought the ashtray out to the kitchen and stopped every now and then to take a restorative, businesslike drag on our cigarettes. There are things women agree on or don't agree on when they work together in this way—whether it is all right to smoke, for instance, or preferable not to in case some

59

migratory ash might find its way onto a clean dish, or whether every single thing that has been on the table has to be washed, whether it has been used or not—and it turned out that Alfrida and I agreed. Also, the thought that I could get away, once the dishes were done, made me feel more relaxed and generous. I had already said that I had to meet a friend that afternoon.

"These are pretty dishes," I said. They were cream-coloured, almost yellowish, with a rim of blue flowers.

"Well, they were my mother's wedding dishes," Alfrida said. "That was one other good thing your grandma did for me. She packed up all my mother's dishes and put them away until the time came when I could use them. Jeanie never knew they existed. They wouldn't have lasted long, with that bunch."

Jeanie. That bunch. Her stepmother and the half brothers and sisters.

"You know about that, don't you?" Alfrida said. "You know what happened to my mother?" Of course I knew. Alfrida's mother had died when an oil lamp exploded in her hands—that is, she died of the burns she got when a lamp exploded in her hands—and my aunts and my mother had spoken of this regularly. Nothing could be said about Alfrida's mother or about Alfrida's father, and very little about Alfrida herself without that death being dragged in and tacked onto it. It was the reason that Alfrida's father left the farm (somewhat of a downward step morally, if not financially). It was a reason to be desperately careful with coal oil, and a reason to be grateful for electricity, whatever the cost. And it was a dreadful thing for a child of Alfrida's age, whatever. (That is—whatever she had done with herself since.)

If it hadn't've been for the thunderstorm she wouldn't ever have been lighting a lamp in the middle of the afternoon.

She lived all that night and the next day and the next night, and it would have been the best thing in the world for her if she hadn't've.

Just the year after that the Hydro came down their road, and they didn't have the need of the lamps anymore.

The aunts and my mother seldom felt the same way about anything, but they shared a feeling about this story. The feeling was in their voices whenever they said Alfrida's mother's name. The story seemed to be a horrible treasure to them, a distinction our family alone could claim. To listen to them had always made me feel as if there were some obscene connivance going on, a fond fingering of whatever was grisly or disastrous.

Men were not like this, in my experience. Men looked away from frightful happenings as soon as they could and behaved as if there were no use, once things were over with, in mentioning them or thinking about them ever again. They didn't want to stir themselves up, or stir other people up.

So if Alfrida was going to talk about it, I thought, what a good thing it was that my fiancé had not come. What a good thing that he didn't have to hear about Alfrida's mother, on top of finding out about my mother and my family's relative—or maybe considerable—poverty. He admired opera and Laurence Olivier's Hamlet, but he had no time for the squalour of tragedy in ordinary life. His parents were healthy and good-looking and prosperous (though he said, of course, that they were dull) and it seemed that he had not had to know anybody who did not live in fairly sunny circumstances. Failures in life—failures of luck, of health, of finances—all struck him as lapses, and his resolute approval of me did not extend to my ramshackle background.

"They wouldn't let me in to see her, at the hospital," Alfrida said, and at least she was saying this in her normal voice, not preparing the way with any greasy tone of piety. "Well, I probably wouldn't have let me in, either, if I'd been in their shoes. I've no idea what she looked like. Probably all bound up like a mummy. Or if she wasn't she should have been. I wasn't there when it happened. I was at school. It got very dark, and the teacher turned the lights on—we had the electric lights, at school—and we all had to stay until the thunderstorm was over. Then my Aunt Lily—well, your grandmother—she came to meet me and took me to her place. And I never got to see my mother again."

I thought that that was all she was going to say, but in a moment she continued, in a voice that had actually brightened up a bit, as if she were preparing for a laugh.

"I yelled and yelled my fool head off. I wanted to see her. I carried on and carried on, and finally, when they couldn't shut me up, your grandmother said to me, 'You're just better off not to see her. You wouldn't want to see her, if you knew what she looks like now. You wouldn't want to remember her this way.' I guess I already knew that she was going to die, because it didn't seem strange to me to hear her talk about remembering her. But you know what I said? I remember saying it. I said, 'But she would want to see me.' *She would want to see me.*"

Then Alfrida really did laugh, or made a snorting sound that was evasive and scornful.

"I must've thought I was the cat's pjs, mustn't I? *She would want to see me.*"

This was a part of the story that I had never heard.

And the minute that I heard it, something happened. It was as if a trap had snapped shut to hold these words in my head. I did not exactly understand what use I would have for them. I knew only how they jolted me and released me, right away, to breathe a different kind of air, available only to myself.

She would want to see me.

The story I wrote, with these words in it, would not exist until years later, not until it had become quite unimportant to think about who had put the idea into my head in the first place.

I thanked Alfrida. I said that I had to go. Alfrida went to call Bill to say goodbye to me, but came back to report that he had fallen asleep.

"He'll be kicking himself when he wakes up," she said. "He enjoyed meeting you."

She took off her apron and accompanied me all the way down the outside steps. At the bottom of the steps was a gravel path leading around to the sidewalk. The gravel crunched under our feet, and she stumbled in her thin-soled house shoes.

She said, "Ouch. God damn it," and caught hold of my shoulder.

"How's your dad?" she said.

"He's all right."

"He works too hard."

I said, "He has to."

"Oh, I know. And how's your mother?"

"She's about the same."

She turned aside, toward the shop window.

"Who do they think is ever going to buy this junk? Look at that honey pail. Your dad and I used to take our lunch to school in pails just like that."

"So did I," I said.

"Did you?" She squeezed me. "You tell your folks I'm thinking about them, will you do that?"

Alfrida did not come to my father's funeral. I wondered if that was because she did not want to see me. As far as I knew, she had never made public what she held against me. But my father had known about it. When I was home visiting him and learned that Alfrida was living not far away—in my grandmother's house, in fact, which she had inherited—I had suggested that we go to see her. This was in the flurry between my two marriages, when I was in an expansive mood, newly released and able to make contact with anyone I chose.

My father said, "Well, you know, Alfrida was a bit upset."

He was calling her Alfrida now. When had that started?

I could not even think, at first, what Alfrida might be upset about. My father had to remind me of the story, published several years ago, and I was surprised, even impatient and a little angry, to think of Alfrida's objecting to something that seemed now to have so little to do with her.

"It wasn't Alfrida at all," I said to my father. "I changed it. I wasn't even thinking about her, it was a character. Anybody could see that."

But, as a matter of fact, there was still the exploding lamp, the mother in her charnel wrappings, the staunch bereft child.

"Well," my father said. He was in general quite pleased that I had become a writer, but he had some reservations about what might be called my character. About the fact that I had ended my marriage for personal—that is, wanton—reasons, and about the way I went around justifying myself, or

63

perhaps, as he might have said, weaselling out of things. But he would not say so—it was not his business anymore.

I asked him how he knew that Alfrida felt this way.

He said, "A letter."

A letter, though they lived not far apart. I did feel sorry to think that he had had to bear the brunt of what could be taken as my thoughtlessness, or even my wrongdoing. Also that he and Alfrida seemed now to be on such formal terms. I wondered what he was leaving out. Had he felt compelled to defend my writing to Alfrida, as he had to other people? He would do that now, though it was never easy for him. In his uneasiness, he might have said something harsh.

There was a danger whenever I was on home ground. It was the danger of seeing my life through someone else's eyes— comparing it, even, with the rich domesticity of others, their pileup production of hand-knitted garments and buttery cakes. Of seeing my own work as ever-increasing rolls of inky-black barbed wire—intricate, bewildering, uncomforting. So that it might become harder to say that writing was worth the trouble.

Worth my trouble, maybe, but what about anyone else's?

My father had said that Alfrida was living alone now. I asked him what had become of Bill. He said that all of that was outside his jurisdiction. But he believed that there had been a bit of a rescue operation.

"Of Bill? How come? Who by?"

"Well, I believe there was a wife."

"I met him at Alfrida's once. I liked him."

"People did. Women."

I had to consider that the rupture might have had nothing to do with me. My father had remarried, and my stepmother had urged him into a new sort of life. They went bowling and curling and regularly joined other couples for coffee and doughnuts at Tim Hortons. She had been a widow for a long time before she married him, and she had many friends from those days who became new friends for him. What had happened with him and Alfrida might have been simply one of the changes, the wearing out of old attachments, that I understood so well in my own life but did not expect to happen in

64

the lives of older people—particularly in the lives of people at home.

My stepmother died just a little while before my father. After their short, happy marriage, they were sent to separate cemeteries to lie beside their first, more troublesome partners. Before either of those deaths, Alfrida had moved back to the city. She didn't sell my grandmother's house; she just went away and left it. "That's a pretty funny way of doing things," my father wrote to me.

There were a lot of people at my father's funeral, a lot of people I didn't know. A woman came across the grass at the cemetery to speak to me. I thought at first that she must have been a friend of my stepmother's. Then I saw that the woman was only a few years past my own age. The stocky figure and puffed-up, hairdresser-blond curls and floral-patterned jacket made her look older.

"I recognized you by your picture," she said. "Alfrida used to always be bragging about you."

I said, "Alfrida's not dead, is she?"

"Oh, no," the woman said, and went on to tell me that Alfrida was in a nursing home in a town just north of Toronto.

"I moved her down there so's I could keep an eye on her."

Now it was easy to tell—even by her voice—that she was somebody of my own generation, and it came to me that she must be a member of the other family, a half sister of Alfrida's, born when Alfrida was almost grownup.

She told me her name, and it was of course not the same as Alfrida's—she must have married. And I couldn't recall Alfrida's ever having mentioned any of her half family by their first names.

I asked how Alfrida was, and the woman said, Cataracts in both eyes, but when they ripened they could be taken off. And she had a serious kidney problem, which meant that she had to be on dialysis twice a week.

"Other than that?" she said, and laughed. I thought, Yes, a sister, because I could hear something of Alfrida in that reckless tossed laugh.

"So she doesn't travel too good," she said. "Or else I

65

would've brought her. She still gets the paper from here, and I read it to her sometimes, and that's where I saw about your dad."

I wondered out loud, impulsively, if I should go to visit, at the nursing home. The emotions of the funeral—all the warm and relieved and reconciled feelings opened up in me by the death of my father at a reasonable age—prompted this suggestion. It would have been hard to carry out. My husband—my second husband—and I were flying to Europe in two days on an already delayed holiday.

"I don't know if you'd get so much out of it," the woman said. "She has her good days. Then she has her bad days. You never know. Sometimes I think she's putting it on. Like, she'll sit there all day and whatever anybody says to her, she'll just say the same thing. 'Fit as a fiddle and ready for love.' That's what she'll say all day long. 'Fit as a fiddle and ready for love.' She'd drive you crazy. Then, other days, she can answer all right."

Again, the woman's voice and laugh, this time half submerged, reminded me of Alfrida's, and I said, "You know, I must have met you. I remember once, when I was over at my grandmother's house and Alfrida's stepmother and her father dropped in, or maybe it was only her father and some of the children—"

"Oh, that's not who I am," the woman said. "You thought I was Alfrida's sister? Glory. I must be looking my age."

I started to say that I could not see her very well, and it was true. In October, the afternoon sun was low, and it was coming straight into my eyes. The woman was standing against the light, so that it was hard to make out her features or her expression.

She twitched her shoulders nervously and importantly. She said, "Alfrida was my birth mom."

Mawm. Mother.

Then she told me, at not too great length, the story that she must have told often, because it was about an emphatic event in her life and an adventure that she had embarked on alone. She had been adopted by a family in eastern Ontario—they were the only family she had ever known ("and I love them

66

dearly")—and she had married and had her children, who were grownup before she got the urge to find out who her own mother was. It wasn't too easy, because of the way records used to be kept, and the secrecy ("It was kept 100% secret that she had me"), but a few years ago she had tracked down Alfrida.

"Just in time, too," she said. "I mean, it was time somebody came along to look after her. As much as I can."

I said, "I never knew."

"No. Those days, I don't suppose too many did. They warn you, when you start out to do this, it could be a shock when you show up. Older people, it's still heavy-duty. But I don't think she minded. Earlier on, maybe she would have."

There was a sense of triumph about the woman, which wasn't hard to understand. If you have something to tell that will stagger someone, and you've told it, and it has done that, you must experience a balmy moment of power. In this case, it was so complete that she felt a need to apologize.

"Excuse me, talking all about myself and not saying how sorry I am about your dad."

I thanked her.

"You know, Alfrida told me that your dad and her were walking home from school one day—this was in high school. They couldn't walk all the way together because, you know, in those days, a boy and a girl, they would just get teased something terrible. So if he got out first he'd wait just where their road went off the main road, outside of town, and if she got out first she would do the same, wait for him. And one day they were walking together and they heard all the bells starting to ring and you know what that was? It was the end of the First World War."

I said that I had heard that story too. "Only I thought they were just children."

"Then how could they be coming home from high school, if they were just children?"

I said that I had thought they were out playing in the fields. "They had my father's dog with them. He was called Mack."

"Maybe they had the dog, all right. Maybe he came to meet

67

them. I wouldn't think she'd get mixed up on what she was telling me. She was pretty good on remembering anything that involved your dad."

Now I was aware of two things. First, that my father had been born in 1902, and that Alfrida was close to the same age. So it was much more likely that they were walking home from high school than that they were playing in the fields, and it was odd that I had never thought of that before. Maybe they had said they were in the fields, that is, walking home across the fields. Maybe they had never said "playing."

Also, that the feeling of apology or friendliness, the harmlessness that I had felt in this woman a little while before, was not there now.

I said, "Things get changed around."

"That's right," the woman said. "People change things around. You want to know what Alfrida said about you?"

Now. Now.

"What?"

"She said you were smart but you weren't ever quite as smart as you thought you were."

I made myself keep looking into the dark face against the light. Smart, too smart, not smart enough. Joke on you.

I said, "Is that all?"

"Except she said you were a cold fish, sort of. That's her talking, not me. I haven't got anything against you."

That Sunday, after the lunch at Alfrida's, I set out to walk all the way back to my rooming-house. Walking both ways, I reckoned that I would cover about ten miles, which ought to offset the effects of the meal I had eaten. I felt over-full, not just of food but of everything that I had seen and sensed in the apartment. The crowded, old-fashioned furnishings. Bill's silences. Alfrida's love, stubborn as sludge, and inappropriate, and hopeless—as far as I could see—on the ground of age alone.

After I had walked for a while, my stomach did not feel so heavy. I made a vow not to eat anything for the next 24 hours. I walked north and west, north and west, on the streets of the tidily rectangular small city. On a Sunday afternoon, there was

68

hardly any traffic, except on the main thoroughfares. A bus might go by with only two or three people in it. People I did not know and who did not know me. What a blessing.

I had lied. I was not meeting any friend. My friends had mostly gone home to wherever they lived. My fiancé would be away until the next day—he was visiting his parents, in Cobourg, on the way home from Ottawa. There would be nobody in the rooming-house when I got there—nobody I had to bother talking or listening to. I had nothing to do.

When I had walked for over an hour, I saw a drugstore that was open. I went in and had a cup of coffee. The coffee was reheated, black and bitter—its taste was medicinal, exactly what I needed. I was already feeling relieved, and now I began to feel happy. Such happiness, to be alone. To see the hot, late-afternoon light on the sidewalk outside, the branches of a tree just out in leaf, throwing their skimpy shadows. To hear from the back of the shop the sounds of the ballgame that the man who had served me was listening to on the radio. I did not think of the story that I would write about Alfrida—not of that in particular—but of the work I wanted to do, which seemed more like grabbing something out of the air than like constructing stories. The cries of the crowd came to me like big heartbeats, full of sorrows. Lovely, formal-sounding waves, with their distant, almost inhuman assent and lamentation.

This was what I wanted, this was what I thought I had to pay attention to, this was how I wanted my life to be.

My White Planet

Mark Anthony Jarman

Whether one marries or not, one lives to regret it—French proverb.

Like watching television, everything coming to us through TV (perhaps why they call it a tube). Seasick gazing on this oyster-white young woman being thrown around like so much thumping laundry.

Her enclosed boat a tiny orange orb among monstrous green icebergs, and I dream of her coming to me, waves like giant white gnashing horses, a female coming like a coma, a young woman staring at me from wild water spray, sliding in and out of sight, her little boat a dizzy dome with plastic windows, an offshore oil-rig's emergency lifeboat, an orange plastic cask bobbing and rolling at the same time.

A final golden vision of her at a microphone, many microphones aimed at her, rented jewels on her sunny neck.

I dream of her and then she is really here, inside a bubble boat, closer and closer to seven of us stumbling on the shingle beach (there used to be more of us, but the bears snatched one and the ice opened and took two), this garden of stone and ice abutting water's wind-wrenched green map, our world a snapping laundry line, her clothes stripped from her and floating in the corner and her marble white body washing and tossing inside an enclosed self-righting lifeboat, arms out, hair askew, awash in icy seawater, an orphan under glass.

Seven of us examine her. Seven men and our Snow White. Her palms turned out, shoulders back, wet dark hair over a freckled white face, and breasts that fit a teacup (we have no teacups here). We touch her neat ribs to hear a heart song, no heat there, navel like a slot for a dime, her thin legs in an

elongated V. The first female for a long time, the first not on
TV from the south, and so cold, yet clearly alive.

You imagine your hands moving up those ribs, pulled to
teacup breasts, warming her, saving her, her dripping skin,
our baggy pants, every man up straight as an icicle, not sure of
her age, what is allowed here.

We inhabit a line station secretly functioning after the accord,
but something went dead after June 11. Our dishes and
software seem without flaw, but our screens remain blank,
thoughtless. No printouts. No officiant plies us with coded
orders or fervent denials or demands our narrow circumspect
data. Is everyone erased in a war or did a budget-conscious
computer take us out in a bureaucratic oversight? We are paid
puppets, but no-one is pulling the strings and no cheque is in
the mail.

The freezing girl is alive but unconscious, and our ungenerous
God has delivered a delirious female to our ice garden where
we look at each other in wonder, wondering about things,
about our farmgirl concubine with drained lips, our charcoal-
eyed dreamgirl, our homage, our stockpiled ohmage.

Peter the Preacher pulls out his blue-grey Czech pistol, says
he'll shoot us or kill her rather than let her be touched, and we
know what he means, means our ugly paws on her lily white
flesh other than to save her, resurrect her, and I believe I once
dreamed this part too, saw Peter the Preacher's fine skull and
fine rhetoric and his fine Czech pistol at our nostril hairs.

Our long lost daughter, we decide, yes, our very sad orphan,
why, our very own child, we all agree at gunpoint, no monkey
business, the Greenland radio-man hard against her belly, me
hard against the small of her back, our honeymoon, our blood
raised, swollen cocks lifted on each side of her, raising her back
to life one degree at a time with just our body heat, one cell at
a time, hours at gunpoint, three crushed in one cot, Peter
never sleeping, her eyes fluttering, legs relaxed, her hair
soaked, mustached men in tears, in blanket memory of past
and future sex, life or death, no monkey business, wanting her
to live, and wanting to be in her, to slide in and out like a

wave, the head so near to her, but instead a Czech pistol, a white towel drying her hair and shoulders and our two ungainly bodies clamped close until her body temperature climbs.

I agree with Peter the Preacher out of selfishness really; I want her for me or for no-one, don't want all their chapped hands on her blue route-map of veins and fine skin. I choose no-one on her, will take my lottery chances for later. Like our red barrels of fuel. They will run out someday, then we must find an alternative or freeze to death. Doc can calculate exactly how long the barrels will last, how long we will last, but as with long-range winter forecasts, some knowledge we'd rather avoid.

We have bears, a few bullets, bubble gum, oatmeal, flour, raisins, dried fruit, lentils, juice crystals, beef jerky, powdered milk, vitamins, chocolate, no dawn, no real fruit, tea with cane sugar, pressed arctic flowers we were told not to pick, but so many blossoms spill over our cliffs in the ceaseless wind.

We carried her from the beach to shelter, my hand inside her senseless scentless thigh, happy to carry her; we were serious and happy, her skin ice-water tight, her hip, her perfect white shores, her ears seeming to listen to us grunting. Our duty, the feel of her leg in my hand, her ear by Rasmussen's hip, dead serious, and much later her dark Acadian eyes gleaming into life, taking in our world, two pin-stars of light suddenly alive in each chocolate brown iris.

Now in the afternoons I read to her, our orphan, from old British picture books and periodicals. She is a blank slate for me to write on, to create.

These are farmkids chasing a greased pig.
This is a bi-plane.
This is a black bathing-suit, a red guitar.
This diamond ring.

We used to explore on the yellow skidoo, but a polar bear ate the fake leather seat (and ate Caird), and on the ice we ran out of oil and blew the whining engine. My hands black trying to find the problem, the carb in pieces, my fingers freezing and filthy. White polar bears after us all the time here—you have to keep an eye out or you're a dead man. Like Caird, pieces of him missing and pieces of him still there, life not the sharp apple it was yesterday.

We found a wooden ship on our lost satellite, stuck in ice, perhaps beached deliberately centuries before, lost men, food still on their table. Did the stiff-legged bears pick them off one by one, eating the years? Slopes of scree and ravens spying on us behind their formal wear, their Aztec razor faces.

I walk her to the wooden ship, as if we are courting, to show her the frozen Norwegian rat lying on ballast stones, stones and rats been there so long a time, born in Europe, Eurocentric rats, going nowhere now.

Have you been here almost as long? she wonders.

We keep the girl alive: she has no memory, learns the world from us, from me. A polar bear circles our camp, its feet huge and almost square, and I can't get over feeling it's a person in a costume. Two bears stalk us; we're bi-polar.

Preacher shot a bear last year and Gingras died after frying the liver with some wild bulbs. For the bears we have rubber bullets and cayenne and skunk spray and even angel dust. We're an experiment. Gingras taught us to not eat the liver.

Our pool table was shipped in, piece by piece, back when there was budget, someone cutting cheques. The way they carted beautiful mahogany bars and mirrors and billiard tables up the western rivers and over the badlands. Up the stone coast I discovered a U-boat weather signal left here during WWII and still transmitting, but our e-mail is broken down. Your Reich takes a hike, your salad days turn Turk. You get depressed, run out of duct tape.

Nothing over satellite anymore, food stopped in our mouth as the satellite feed stopped: no death star, no blues channel, no idea what's out there still. May 1st brought brief pictures of

Ho Chi Minh, stigmata, a Warhol banana, an AK-47. What's happening out there past the clouds of mosquitoes?

We play cards: Go Fish, War, 45, High Chicago, Low Chicago, five-card, seven-card. For exercise I jump on the tiny round trampoline. Run outside and the arthritic huskies attack you, though they're fine if you walk. Jog and they think they're supposed to kill you, some old instinct they won't let go. Jumping up and down seems good for your cells, plumps them up. You feel better, younger.

An electronic detection system warns us if bears are sneaking close while we're working outside the quonsets with our big hoods up, wind singing loud as jets.

An airplane—a beautiful engine's martial music with dynamic bass boost, silver fuselage, and no insignia, no pilot for all we know, or the pilot dead. A long jet-stream heading to the north pole. The captain runs the rocky guano beach as if he can lasso that damn plane, catch its amplified buzz.

We keep shooting pool, running the table, though I play slop—just hit the balls and see what happens. The captain runs alone, comes back in with cold air hanging in his shirt. We give each other bad haircuts in our hours of darkness. On our beach we hold clear panes of ice overhead and smash them to the ground like breaking glass.

These are prickly hair curlers.
These are pink pedal pushers.
That's green grass.
That's the way a rich woman sits in an Adirondack chair.

Our VCR shows the old football and hockey games over and over, and we bet on them even though we've seen them a million times.
GO! GO! GO!
Blitz! Dog it up the middle.
Eat that blocker. Run!
Get rid of it! Shoot it!
Come to Daddy!

74

Top shelf!
Through the uprights.
Yes. No!
Or a history channel special on Dien Bien Phu, the bearded foreign legions, firebases named after a French officer's mistresses (Eliane, Beatrice, Isabelle, Claudine, Gabrielle...). How lucky the man was, until he shot himself in the bunker in Indochina.

Another dead pilot soars over us, air gone, precision machine on auto, fly till fuel drained, flying on fumes, vapours wavering like ghosts inside steel rivets. And finally down, where no-one witnesses, eight miles high and then that metal skin ripping down to the ice.

Some men in the group have each other; we don't discuss their arrangements, the niceties. You dream of rivers, riding elephants.

I remember childhood fields clad in yellow grain, and they seem surreal. Did I really live there? Was the farm real? Such livid yellow blue red green and that Hutterite vibe. This ice the only real world, an afterlife, *on ice*, but the only world that counts.

In our afterlife she tries to sweep the rug wearing my white shirt, my shirt you can see through and her blue pedal pushers made of my cut-off longjohns, shrunken from being washed, holding tighter and tighter, and she's bending at the gentle broom and I can't help but look on the cant and lexicon of her lovely lines and want to be all things to all people.

I am given to bad dreams, am the bearer of bad news, prophet of grim gesture.
I begin carving Rasmussen a Celtic Cross, his gravestone, his dark green-eyed soapstone rood.

These are bottles of stout.
These are shopping malls.
These are car dealers.
Freeways and doom palms.

Gambling is the only way we make our randomly picked taped games more interesting, but then one fine Sunday our VCR breaks, movies flipping, eating game tapes.

Try tracking!

I tried it goddamit! You try fuckin' tracking!

We clean the dirty VCR with virginal movies we never watch: *Ma & Pa Kettle, Snow White*, training films. Our cranky VCR works for a while, we're happy again, then nothing again. Snow so industrious on the screen.

We look at each other, lost, no words, byzantine in ardour, drooping with anger. Time does not equal money.

Rasmussen's idea. The VCR dead. Everyone could have equal chits, Rassy says, have turns with her. And you can gamble your turn to be with her, lose or win, move a finger slowly, summon honey from her, and she can be Eve, create a new race.

Our faces change. I knew this was coming.

What's wrong with that? he protests. The old rules don't apply here. What if everyone is gone? You know, out there. Maybe she'll like it. You'd like it. You think anyone would do what we've done so far? Been good. We've been stupid. Why can't we just do what we want?

We have all thought about trying it. I remember lying beside her at gunpoint to bring her to life, our orphan, our animal heat on both sides of her, my cock up against her white marble hip, its head also marble, a taut gleaming bulb, seeking my orphan, remembering her form, knowing her without knowing her. What I would pay to put it in, but we did not. Our daughter, our sister, the only woman we know. Who would be first? Who would explain? Me?

We were happier before Rasmussen brought this up again. We thought it had been decided that she didn't really exist. Instantly her hips and breasts suggest their shape to us through Gore-Tex or wool or cotton (*cotton kills*), suggest intriguing possibilities.

She brings us tea in the same battered tin pot but it is different now. We are secret czars of romance, closet Rasputins, long johns too small on her hips, clinging in pleasant lines that draw your eye down and in, show exact aspects of her female anatomy. Not every woman does that; she has that special look, that power. Sometimes she kisses us, sometimes she studies us, one after the other. What does she think?

Our radar spinning madly, the dish silent. We all know he's right. We are so alive. Fuck I hate Rassy.

Wear these snow pants, I say to her.
They smell like diesel, she says.
Wear them, I say.
What's wrong with these? she asks.
Wear these over them.

We shun Rasmussen for seven weeks; he slips and gets a concussion and can't get around, but still we won't speak to him.
You know I'm only saying what you all thought.
I think of her on her stomach, sunlight in her room, a liaison as if in a city, my fingers moving slowly up her legs, sunlight in her room, moving all around, but waiting, moving up around her ribcage and cupping her in front, my dreamgirl waiting for me, open and smooth. I can't get her out of my head. We shun him.

We play music from the University of the Air tapes, the history of rock and roll, scribble extensive notes on Johnny Horton's blue period, Otis Blackwell doing "Pictures of Matchstick Men," Calexico's Spanish horn, Ray Price's crazy arms that long to hold somebody new, Jack Nitzsche's "The Lonely Surfer." Only I remember Jack's pistol pushing into the movie star, Jack's work with Neil Young, "Whiskey Boot Hill," and Graham Parker's best LP, *Squeezing Out Sparks*. Whatever happened to lucky Lene Lovitch?
"Do you have to breathe so loudly?!"
"Are we out of salt?!"
No new music here, no murky swamp rock, no psychobilly, though a rich fantasy life. Where her legs meet, hidden under the longjohns. We are swathed always in layers, you get used

77

to layers, masks for outside when it's bad, never completely warm.

Rasmussen says, *I may be gone some time,* edges out into the blizzard with his flowering concussion.

Our talks continue. She sits by me, her body so warm.

These are lawyers.
These are debutantes.
These are power lines.
This is a sizzling steak.

I find his frozen body, arm up with no glove.

We make brief contact with a woman in the Outback. She pedals a bike to power an old ham radio. She is never cold there, a woman's skin painted with sweat all day. We are connected, then lose her, but we know the world is still out there.

Our two bears off somewhere hunting for tasty seals in slob ice and slush. We stand around the solar collector, drop our pants and show white asses, reflecting extra light into the panel. This display of white skin seems to make all the difference for our patched up equipment.

First a video channel, then a shopping channel. Ads for heroic pickup trucks bashing and splashing through rivers, the mad colours of a lost world. When did I last drive anything with wheels and a heater? Did the world go away or did we? Its whisper-quiet ride, its no money down o.a.c.

The world seems ridiculous, but she watches the miraculous screen, fascinated. My old tracksuits have surfaced in Glasgow. She watches videos with tall models and turquoise swimming pools; she learns songs, takes on new moves, mannerisms, dances in her socks (*my socks!*). She is in love. After a while she doesn't really want to read books with me, *sorry,* doesn't really want to walk to our wooden ship, doesn't find our dead rat romantic.

A big boat with a stripe the red of lipstick used to call once a year. A mistake to mention it. A risk if the weather turns at all bad, in fact a dangerous journey even when conditions are perfect, and they have to be perfect, and they're never perfect. She says she's going to leave, go without me. Polar bears are worse than grizzlies, *meaner*, and they like females. Bears like menstrual blood, are attracted, anarchists wanting under the underwear.

Wind up, forecast bad, we sneak away without word one to the others, knowing we might be dooming ourselves like Rassy, but life is losing, is risk. She wants the world and I want her.

It's uphill and downhill, a plodding broken hike, and unreliable ice in the straits. The two of us follow the old stone cairns, dwarfs in the vast landscape, lunar explorers, endless lost horizon and cliffs like calipers, white mountains, wracked spiny shore, wind penetrating like a wish, but the sky clear and no bears taking a lively interest.

Binoculars and I spy nothing. Sit another day as if at a bus stop in the middle of nowhere wishing I had a cigarette, a rare steak sandwich with a martini, some Sernylan tranq in case we need to shoot a bear. Our backpacks at a sunny bus stop.

She says she sees its smokestack in the bright icebergs. I have my glacier glasses on for the glare. Where? I can't see anything. Are my eyes going? Is she seeing what she wants to see? Is she that lucky?

Bright daytime but I fire the flare and half a day later the confident hull smashing black and white Dalmatian ice just for her, smokestack's lipstick red stripe just for her, ice shot through with zigzags, shadow lines, the ice a white kitchen floor suddenly buckling up, a bright breaking world roaring below sous chefs grinning at the ship's rail and white shag state-rooms where Brooklyn tourists bray *Hope we see a bear!!* Buffets, fresh bread, pepper steak, blueberries, green eyes and the exact shadow of this ship laid on the ice.

Aren't I climbing aboard? she asks me.
What's wrong? she asks.
I give her my Checkers speech.

Mad at how happy she is to leave me in the leads, in the bright shadows of the ship, so white here, can't open both eyes. She tries to give me back my fur hat. No-one will ever know me the way she could have. I am a prince and a janitor both. We killed Rassy because of her.
Keep it, keep the hat.

Once she saw me about to have a shower. I staged it so she could see all of me, her eyes on me better than nothing on me. How strange it is to be alive. The men talk of tracing energy files, of molecular vibrations, molecular mechanics. Laughing, the men talk of the guy back home who could leap from inside one 45 gallon drum into another and do a flip without even a step and jumped right over a stock car to punch the driver, and Navvy was working the rock crusher and dropped a boulder on the roof of the guy's truck and he jumped out and hit Navvy and Navvy didn't know if it was Christmas or New Year, never been hit so hard, but laughing and proud to have been smacked by this backroader now dead of cancer.

We see her on Infotainment Tonight. She is shacked up with one of Jack Nicholson's sons. They walk on the beach and Junior Jack smiles that rakish smile, light at that magic hour the Arriflex cameras love. The cameras love our dreamgirl and he winks, their teeth white as bears on ice. In her new video she dances with tanned surfers. In late tropical light they all face us, scissor kicks, hair flying, sand flat as a gym floor from water lying over it, the sun going down in her video and she's wearing my white shirt. Water and western sky the colours of deep neon and she's in my shirt.

I remember the naked white body rolling in icy seawater, the window into the self-righting oil rig lifeboat, that window like a TV and we stared in like the bears stare in at us. Outside that window it's death. I thought I could teach her.

I feel everything is over now, I feel so ordinary without her. It's like missing yourself and maybe one thing waiting.

Her sodden hair and skin, that naked ass coming up into view like a frozen white planet, my lovely planet, never once touched save to save her, to carry her. Escaped—air we can't breathe. Would it have been so bad to breathe of her? Would the world have ended?

I looked at her in her sleep, half out of her army bag, that white hip, and I pulled her underwear down on one side just to see what she looked like. Shaking I was so tense and she was sleeping, dead to the world after walking with me all day. She lives because of us and even though she's gone I own her.

In the cold hangars and quonsets we're down to the last barrels of naptha, diesel (someone is sniffing it), the last juice crystals while on the cruise ship they eat strawberries from Mexico. I could always fry up some liver I suppose, end it all, but I like it here, these contorted icefields have become my vast home. Home is a strange pliable word, the world in a snapping laundry line, your mother a giant in blue sky, Adam and Eve now gone from the postwar suburb. Exactly how little you need—I'm still waiting to find that out.

After she gets out some of the others won't wait anymore. We argue about it. They're mad I left. They're mad I came back. The Greenland radio-man and Doc the chess master-machinist decide on overland. Sayonara, adieu to you and you.

They're gone. They haven't made it, haven't made it on TV. Bad sign.

At the Emmys she gives us a message. Big hi to the seven dwarves if they're watching; they'll know who they are. A little laugh, her tiny dress taped to her skin to keep it on while we wear more layers to stretch the fuel. On a screen she has so much presence, light, heat. Here she seemed smaller walking in this endless landscape. Her newest boyfriend wears my fur hat. It's trendy. People on the screen seem happy, coloured cars everywhere. What would I do in that world? Miss this one?

I jump on my tiny trampoline, do pushups, fat boiling on burner, eating shorebirds when I can catch them. We are alone up here, we're watching out for those two polar bears. They want us, they love us so much, and they do anything they want.

We make noise at the front door and the two bears run happily to catch us in their embrace and then one of us scoots out the back door to the next building. If they ever figure out the two doors we're dead. We have skunk spray, slink around, not sure how well it works.

I am proud of our frozen girl, in a way glad our starlet hasn't told, hasn't sent anyone to find our listening post where we don't listen.

The bears, when they stand erect, are tall enough to peer in any of our windows. White mountains far away, and dark lines of whalebone scrimshaw. Where are my hallucinatory fields of yellow and purple?

Sharpening a hacksaw in a visegrip, I look up and see the bear staring in at me, its long neck extended earnestly, black paw pads, black nose, squinty black eyes hiding in that expanse of white rug *(and I think of her naked on a fireside rug, bearskin, jealous of Malibu, the old highway)*. A window ten feet off the ground and I am on display like a lobster in a restaurant.

The bear looks goofy standing up, a carnival act, arms out, a myopic giant trying to balance on two legs with this doofus expression: *Hey Ma, look at me!*

They know us, big carnal carnivores peeking in at our parts. They spy us in the window and are nostalgic for the happy future when they will have us in their arms.

What Saffi Knows

Carol Windley

That summer a boy went missing from a field known as the
old potato farm, although no-one could remember anything
growing there but wild meadow barley, thistles in their mul-
titudes, black lilies with a stink of rotten meat if you brought
your face too close or tried to pick them. There were white
fawn lilies like stars fallen to earth and bog-orchids, also called
candle-scent, and stinging nettles, blameless to look at, leaves
limp as flannel, yet caustic and burning to the touch. Even so,
nettle leaves could be brewed into a tea that acted on the system like a tonic, or so Saffi's aunt told her. She recited a little
rhyme that went: *Nettle tea in March, mugwort leaves in May and
all the fine maidens will not go to clay.*

Picture a field, untended, sequestered, grass undulating in a
fitful wind. Then disruption, volunteer members of the search
party arriving, milling around, uniformed police and tracking
dogs, distraught relatives of the missing boy. No place for a
child, Saffi's mother said, yet here Saffi was, holding tight to
her Aunt Loretta's hand, taking everything in.

All the people were cutout dolls. The sun hovered above the
trees like a hot-air balloon cut free. Saffi's shoes were drenched
from walking in the wet grass; she was wearing a sundress
that tied at the back of her neck and she kept scratching at
mosquito bites on her arms and legs until they bled and her
Aunt Loretta said she'd give herself blood poisoning, but Saffi
didn't stop, she liked how it felt, it gave her something to do.
She could see her daddy, standing a little apart from the others, drinking coffee from a paper cup. He was a young man
then, tall, well-built, his hair a sprightly reddish-brown, his

head thrown back, eyes narrowed in concentration, as if he hoped to be first to catch sight of any unusual movement in the woods, down near the river. Saffi looked where he was looking and saw a flitting movement in the trees like a turtledove, its silvery wings spread like a fan and its voice going coo-coo, the sound a turtledove would make when it was home and could rest at last. But there was no turtledove. Never would there be a turtledove. Saffi was the only one who knew the truth, part of the truth. The only one. She knew something. But who would listen to her? Who would believe? What was true and what was something else, a made-up story?

July 1964, in a town on Vancouver Island, in the days before the tourists and land developers arrived, when it was still quiet and everyone more or less knew everyone else. There was a pulp and paper mill, a harbour where the fishing fleet tied up, churches, good schools, neighbourhoods where children played unsupervised. Children were safe in this town. They did not go missing. But unbelievably not one but two children were gone, one for nearly six weeks and then three days ago this other boy, his red three-speed bike found ditched at the edge of the old potato farm, where it seemed he liked to play, hunting snakes and butterflies, but never hurting anything, never causing any trouble, just catching things and letting them go.

His name was Eugene Dexter. His jacket had been found snagged in a hawthorn tree beside the Millstone River, at the far end of the old potato farm. Or else it was a baseball cap that was found. Or a catcher's mitt. You heard different stories. There was a ransom note. There was no such note. The police had a suspect, or, alternately, they had no suspects, although they'd questioned and released someone and were refusing to give out details. But, said Saffi's mother, wasn't that how they operated, secretly, out of the public eye, trying to conceal their own ineptness? She kicked at a pebble. A woman standing beside her said she'd had a premonition and showed the gooseflesh on her arms. Some men got into a scrum, like elderly, underfed rugby players, and began praying aloud.

84

One minute it was warm and then a sudden cold wind would make Saffi shiver. Behind the mountain dark clouds welled up, filled with a hidden, shoddy light. The boy's parents arrived in a police car, lights flashing. But maybe Saffi was remembering that wrong. Maybe they drove up in their own car, Mr. Dexter behind the wheel. In any case, there they were, Mr. and Mrs. Dexter, making their way over to tables borrowed from the high school cafeteria and set up in the field, with plates of donuts and fresh coffee and mimeographed instructions for the search party, so perhaps it wasn't surprising when Arthur Dawsley sidled up to Saffi's mother and said it was quite the three-ring circus, wasn't it, quite the shindig. Arthur Dawsley lived next door to Saffi's house, behind a hedge, behind a fence, in a garden full of flowers. When Saffi was learning to talk she'd mispronounced his name, saying Arthur Daisy, and in her family it was the wrong name that stuck. It didn't suit him; she wished she could take it back. Her parents teased her, calling Arthur Daisy her friend, but he wasn't. His hair the colour of a cooking pot was in deep waves above his forehead. Under his windbreaker he was wearing a white shirt and a tie. He said he knew it was no circus, that was merely a figure of speech and not a good one, considering. He was too old to be of much help, he supposed, but surely he could lend a little moral support. Surely he could.

"Beautiful weather, all the same," he said, and then he walked in his peculiar upright stolid fashion over to Saffi's daddy, who averted his face slightly and emptied the dregs of his coffee onto the ground, as if the last thing in the world he craved was a word with Arthur Daisy. And at the same time the boy's father was handing an item of clothing over to the police, a green striped soccer shirt, it looked like, tenderly folded, and the police let their dogs sniff it and they strained at their leashes as if they'd been given a new idea and the sound of their baying came like a cheerless chorus off the mountain.

Later the wind died down and the clouds built up, dark clouds edged with a beautiful translucent white, dazzling to the eye, and just as Saffi and her mother and aunt got in the car to go home there was a violent drenching downpour, and everyone would say it was almost a relief, it was turning out to be such a hot, dry summer.

This could be said of her: she was a child who noticed things, who took things in, and she could never decide, was this a curse or a gift? A curse, she thought, for the most part.

The child she was, the person she would become: in a way they were like two people trapped in the same head. The child mystified her. The child with her pallor, her baby-fine, slightly dry hair, her eyes, heavy-lidded and unusually large, her air of distraction, of fragility and wariness. And her odd little name that her mother had got out of a book: Saffi, meaning "wisdom." *Who are you? I am Saffi, no-one else.* She felt sympathy for the child, of course she did, and affection, impatience, anger, shame. And sorrow. Shouldn't someone have been looking out for her? Shouldn't someone have been watching over her? Daddy's girl, her daddy always called her, but daddy didn't have much time for her, not really.

Mornings, when her aunt was busy doing housework, Saffi waited until Arthur Daisy had left in his car, which he did sometimes, not every day, and then she crawled through a gap in the laurel hedge into his backyard. She knelt in the shade, looking out at the things he kept there: a wheelbarrow tipped up against a garden shed, a pile of buckets, a heap of steamy grass clippings buzzing with bluebottles, a mound of composted dirt he made from dead leaves and garbage from his kitchen, egg shells and potato peelings.

At the foot of the porch steps there was a metal folding chair and an overturned washtub he used as a table, a coffee mug on it. Two of his shirts hung from the clothesline like guards he'd left on duty.

He'd painted his cellar window black, but he'd missed out a little place shaped like a star and she could get up close to it and see a shaded light hanging from the ceiling and beneath the light a table with a boy crouched on it. He was a real boy. She saw him and he saw her, his eyes alert and shining, and then he let his head droop on his chest. Don't be scared, she said; don't be. He was awake but sleeping, his arm twitching, his feet curled like a bird's claws on a perch. All she could see in the dim light was his hair, nearly white. He was wearing a pair of shorts.

He was there every day. She called him bird-boy. She whistled at him softly, as if he were a wild thing. She had to be careful. Since he'd got the bird-boy, Arthur Daisy never stayed away for long, he'd drive off and then almost at once he was back, slamming his car door and pounding up the porch steps to his front door. Before he got that far, though, Saffi would have scrambled back through the hedge, her hair catching in the branches, so that she'd have to give it a cruel tug, but she never cried or uttered the least sound, and at last she was home free.

If Arthur Daisy happened to be working in his yard and spotted her playing outside, he'd call to her. "Well, Saffi, what do you think I've got?" he would say. He would open the gate in his fence and tell her to come on over and see.

He looked like the old troll that lived under the bridge in The Three Billy Goats Gruff. He wore an old brown cardigan, the pockets sagging with junk. What do you think I've got, he'd say, and he'd pull something out of a pocket and hold it in his clenched fist and if she stepped back he'd bend closer, closer, his colourless lips drawn back so that she could see his stained teeth, gums the bluish-pink of a dog's gums. She didn't want to guess, she was no good at it. She covered her eyes until he told her to look and it would turn out to be an old nail or a screwdriver or the sharp little scissors he used for cutting roses.

"Well?" he'd say. "What does Saffi know? Has the cat got Saffi's tongue?" He slapped his hand on his trouser leg and laughed his old troll laugh and picked up his shovel and went back to work digging in his garden.

That summer Saffi's mother got hired as an operator at the BC Telephone Co. on Fitzwilliam Street, her first job, she said, since she'd got married. Her first real job, ever. If she had a choice she wouldn't leave Saffi, but the truth was they needed the income; she'd lost interest in being poor her entire life.

She ran up some dresses for work on her old treadle sewing machine, dark blue dresses, in rayon or a serviceable poplin, something she could gussy up with a little white collar or a strand of pearls. Saffi remembered her mother wearing the dresses for years, until they wore out, and then she cut them up and stitched them into a quilt for Saffi, and Saffi had it still, folded away in a cedar chest her husband's parents had given her for a wedding present. When she took it out and ran her fingers over the scraps of fabric, little cornfields, little meadows of blue, she couldn't help remembering those long-ago summer mornings, bright and hot, dreamlike, almost, when she'd clung to her mother and begged her to stay home, and her mother had given her a weary, abstracted glance and pulled on the little chamois-soft gloves she wore for driving and demanded Saffi give her a nice quick kiss goodbye and then she was gone. Saffi couldn't get her breakfast down, her throat ached so much from not letting herself cry. Her aunt rinsed the oatmeal down the drain, what a terrible waste, she said, and then she wiped Saffi's face with a dishrag and sent her outside while she got on with cleaning the house. Saffi sat in the sun on the front steps and looked at a book with pictures of a frog prince, his blubbery mouth pursed for a kiss, a scraggly old witch with skinny fingers reaching out to grab and hold you fast.

Even though she knew he couldn't see her, she imagined the bird-boy was watching and she turned the pages carefully. She was good at reading, but poor at arithmetic. It wasn't her fault. The numbers had their own separate lives, their own shapes, and refused to let her touch them. 9 in its soldier's uniform the colour of an olive with a double row of brass buttons. 3 a Canterbury bell, a curled-up snail leaving a trail of slime, dragging its little clamshell house behind. 7 had a licking tongue of fire and smelled like a thunderstorm. 4 was the sea coming in along the shore, it was a ship sailing, it was blue and white and stood on its one leg.

The numbers said Leave us be! Be quiet! Don't touch! They kept themselves apart, like little wicked soldiers in a castle. The teacher held her worksheets up in class and said, Is this the work a Grade 1 girl should be doing? Saffi had to cover her ears and sing to herself about the Pied Piper, how he made the rats skip after him out of town and then the children followed and the town got dark and the parents lamented, Oh, what have we done?

When Aunt Loretta finished the housework she called Saffi inside and read her a story about a turtledove.

"I know what that is," Saffi said. "I seen a turtledove in the cellar at Arthur Daisy's house."

Aunt Loretta said she must have seen some other kind of bird. "All we have around here is pigeons," she said. "You know what a pigeon looks like, don't you? And it's I saw, not I seen."

"It looked like a boy," Saffi said. "It had white feathers on its head. It sang like this, *cheep, cheep, cheep.*"

"Oh, Saffi," her aunt said. "You are a funny little thing."

Outside her house the road was all churned up where her daddy parked his logging truck when he got home. He'd swing her up into the cab and she'd sit behind the steering-wheel and he'd get her to pretend she was the driver, telling her, "Start the engine, Saffi, or we'll still be sitting here when those logs sprout a whole new set of roots and branches." He made engine noises like a growling cat and she pretended to turn the wheel and he gave directions. "Turn left," he'd say. "Gear down for the hill, now shift into third, that's the way." It was hot in the truck and there was a sour smell of her daddy's sweaty work shirt, stale thermos coffee, engine oil, the beer her daddy drank. Her daddy always said he was a hard-working, hard-drinking man and people could take him or leave him. Leave him, was his preference. He liked a quiet life. He liked his home and when he got home he deserved a beer, didn't he? "Yes," said Saffi. "Yes, sir, you do."

Outside the truck the world sped past, blurred and strange.

Who are you? her daddy said. Are you daddy's girl?

Her daddy. Danny Shaughnessy. He was away in the woods for days at a time, then he'd be home, he'd come into the kitchen, where Saffi was standing on a kitchen chair at the counter, helping Aunt Loretta coat chicken pieces with flour or peel potatoes, little tasks her aunt allotted her to fill in the last hour or so until her mother returned. Her daddy would go straight to the fridge for a beer and sometimes he gave Saffi a taste, the beer making her gag and trickling down her chin and her daddy laughed and kissed it away. Her aunt told him to leave her alone. He said she was his kid, wasn't she?—he didn't have to leave his own kid alone, did he? Then Aunt Loretta said he could at least take off his work boots and wash his hands.

"Don't you have a kitchen of your own to go to?" he'd say. "Isn't it time you got back to good old Vernon, Loretta?"

They fought like kids, the way kids at school went at each other, hands on their hips, faces thrust forward, then they agreed to an armistice and sat at the kitchen table and had a glass of beer together, Saffi with them, and her daddy praised her, saying what a doll she was, a real little lady. On the drive down from Campbell River, he'd heard on the radio a boy was missing, ten years old, a thin boy, with white-blonde hair, when last seen wearing shorts, a blue jacket, running shoes. And then, just south of Royston, a boy who answered that description exactly was standing at the side of the highway and he'd blasted the horn at him, because kids never understood, they had no idea how much room a truck like that needed to stop, they'd run out without thinking. More than likely it was some other kid, but what if it was this Eugene Dexter and he'd just driven on by?

He had another beer. He talked about joining the search party. He had a sense for these things, he said, a kind of infallible sixth sense, which was why he never got lost in the woods or took a wrong turn driving the truck. He stood up and stretched and said he was going to have a shower. What time was supper going to be, he wanted to know, and Aunt Loretta said it would be when it was ready and not a minute before.

"Daddy's girl!" her daddy said, sweeping Saffi off her feet, holding her high above his head, shaking her as if she were a cloth doll, her hair flopping in her eyes, and she laughed so hard she thought her sides would split open and the stuffing would fall out. I'll knock the stuffing out of you, her daddy said when he was angry. But he was teasing. He was never angry with her. She was his girl. He tossed her in the air and caught her safely, every time. His fingers dug hard into her ribs and she couldn't get a breath.

"Can't you see she's had enough," her aunt said.

If she wasn't laughing so hard, if her daddy wasn't laughing and cursing Aunt Loretta, telling her she was a tight-assed old broad, she could tell him she had this bad secret in her head that hurt like blisters from a stinging nettle. In Arthur Daisy's cellar there was a bird-boy, a turtledove, its head tucked beneath its wing.

Sleep, oh, sleep, my turtledove, and in the new day I will come for you.

It seemed to her a line divided her yard from Arthur Daisy's yard. Even after all these years she saw this line as a real thing, like a skipping-rope or a length of clothesline or a whip, taut and then slack, then pulled tight again until it sang like a banjo string and nearly snapped in two. The line or the rope or whatever it was separated the dangerous elements, fire and air, from the more amenable elements of earth and water. That was how she imagined it. She crept into his yard, holding her breath, mouse-y small, so small and quick no-one could catch her. She pressed her hands to the window. She had to see if the bird-boy was still there, perched on his roost. And he was. He scared her to death. His skull was luminous and frail as an egg, yet he seemed strong to her, he seemed the strongest thing, his gaze cold, not beseeching, but full of strength, as if nothing could hurt him. His eyes were dark, like a bird's eyes. What did he eat? Where did he sleep at night? She called to him, whistling a tune she'd made up. She told him not to be afraid. She cupped a black and yellow caterpillar in her hand. It was so small she felt her heart curl around it. She remembered the old hawthorn tree near the river, light spilling in tatters through the leaves, the sun caught fast in its branches. In her mind she saw the boy's jacket hanging there still, as if no-one cared enough to take it home.

She held the caterpillar up to the window, saying, look at this, look at this.

All around there was fire and air, scorching her hair and

clothes, leaving her weak and sick and shaking with a chill, so that her mother would have to put her to bed and take her temperature and fuss over her and say what you done to yourself, Saffi? She put a cold cloth on Saffi's forehead and called her sweet dumpling pie and gave her half a baby Aspirin and a little ginger ale to swallow it with.

What did Saffi see? She saw Arthur Daisy in his garden, snipping at blood-red roses and sprays of spirea, telling Saffi he was on his way to visit the municipal cemetery to put flowers on his mother's grave, his old mother, who'd passed away twenty years ago this month, almost to the day, dead of a wasting disease, did Saffi know what that meant? It ate her body up, her skin, her flesh, and she never was a fleshy person. She shrivelled up to the size of an old lima bean, a mean little midget, a dried pea. She'd scare the liver out of you, he said, and that's a fact. That was what happened when you got to be as old as he was, he told Saffi. You ended up having to visit the dear departed on a regular basis. He put his scissors and cut flowers on the ground.

"What's wrong with you?" he said. "Cat got your tongue, little girl?" He looked at her. He looked into her eyes and she knew he saw everything in her head, how scared she was.

"Well, well," he said, brushing a leaf off his sleeve. "Isn't Saffi a funny little monkey?" he said at last.

Before she could do a thing, run, or squirm out of his reach, he reached out and gave her arm a hard pinch just above her elbow. It burned like a hornet's sting. "There, now," said Arthur Daisy, turning his face away. He picked up his flowers. He pocketed his scissors. Don't think anything, she told herself. Don't think. Behind her in the house there was the bird-boy crouched in the cellar, eating crumbs from the palm of his hand. She saw him like that in her dreams. She couldn't get rid of him.

Sleep: what was *sleep*? Saffi's mother complained that never in her life had she suffered from insomnia, normally she didn't even dream, and now she was lucky if she got two or three hours of decent sleep a night. It could be the heat, she said. Or it could be that her head was crackling with the sound of voices, her own voice repeating endlessly, Number, please, and One moment please, while your call is completed, and then the voices of strangers, people to whom she'd never in this life be able to attach a face or name, endlessly chattering, demanding her time and attention. She wasn't used to working; her nerves were shot. She'd lie awake until dawn, her temples throbbing, and it would seem a feeling of unbearable sadness, of grief, would descend on her and she would imagine herself lost in some outlandish forested place, tripping over roots, trudging up winding paths, slipping down, getting nowhere, calling and calling and no-one answering, although sometimes she saw in the distance the figure of a boy, thin and pale in the encroaching gloom, an unsettling vision from which she couldn't escape. It haunted her all day. She hated this summer. It was an unlucky season; it was a trial to her and everyone else.

Saffi's mother worried about everything, she told Saffi; about life passing her by, not getting the things she'd set her heart on, like a nicer house, with three bedrooms, in case she and Danny decided to have more kids, which they might, a little brother or sister for Saffi, or maybe one of each. Wouldn't that be fun? she said, tugging a comb through the snarls in Saffi's hair. In the mirror her eyes were resolute and bright, the skin around her mouth taut and pale. But Aunt Loretta always said it was her turn. Her turn. Who could doubt her? She had a nursery prepared, the walls papered with kittens tangled up in balls of yarn. There were drawers full of handmade baby clothes and a bassinet with a silk coverlet and when Saffi visited she was allowed to lay her doll in it. Aunt Loretta patted the doll's tummy and said, What a fine baby you have there, and for a moment it truly seemed there was a real baby asleep in the bed, snoring and fat as a little cabbage.

On the drive home in the car, Saffi's mother would say what a shame, what a shame, but not everyone could have what they wanted. She shifted gears with a brisk movement of her wrist. "You can have a perfectly fulfilled life without children. Sometimes I almost wish—." She glanced at herself in the rear-view mirror. "Well," she said. "I wish Loretta luck, that's all." And Saffi understood that her mother didn't want Aunt Loretta to have a baby or anything else, she was afraid Aunt Loretta would use up all the available good luck on herself, the small quantity of it there was in this world, thus stealing something irreplaceable from Saffi's mother. But knowing this didn't make Saffi love her mother less. If anything, it made her love her more, but from a little farther off, like the time her daddy took her to watch Uncle Vernon's team playing baseball and they sat high up in the bleachers and her daddy said they needed high-powered binoculars just to figure out who in the hell was on the pitcher's mound.

You can make your life turn out any way you want, Saffi's mother said.

You can realize your dreams, through persistence and hard work combined with just a smidgen of good fortune, she said. Just a smidgen. That's all I ask.

She drove so fast, barely slowing at stop signs, a police ghost car pulled her over and the officer gave her a ticket and Saffi's mother said, "Not again!" Then she told the police officer he had such a nice smile it was almost worth it. Son of a bitch, she muttered, letting the ticket fall to the floor of the car, where it got ripped in half when Saffi trod on it getting out. Saffi had imagined running to the police officer and saying, Wait, I know where he is, I know where he's hiding, please listen, but she had remained in her seat, glued to the upholstery, the heat making her sweaty and numb, and she'd hated herself, stupid, stupid Saffi, what's the matter, *cat got your tongue?*

"We are all autonomous beings," her mother said. "We all have free will. It's just a matter of waiting for a few lucky breaks, that's all."

Within a very few years, as it turned out, Aunt Loretta and Uncle Vernon were the parents of twin boys, and then they had a baby girl and Saffi had three cousins to help care for, but she never did get the brother or sister her mother had promised her. Life tripped you up. It didn't work out as you expected; it never did. In 1968, when Saffi was eleven, her father was forced to quit work after developing chronic lower back pain, diagnosed variously as a herniated disc, sciatica, an acute inflammation at the juncture of the sacrum and the iliac, perhaps treatable with cortisone, and her father said it was all the same to him, he was fed up with the whole deal. He stayed at home watching TV and staring out the window at the rain, drumming his fingers on the glass, a prisoner, and Saffi's mother would come home from work and grab his prescription drugs up off the kitchen table and say in disgust, "Beer and painkillers? Not that I care. You're not a child, Danny Shaughnessy, are you? You can do what you damned well please."

Her father moved out of the house. He stayed at a dubious-looking motel on the highway and collected sick pay until it ran out, and then he packed up and announced he was moving to Ontario. He said he was no good to anyone and Saffi's mother said she wasn't about to argue the point. His hair was prematurely grey; he walked with the slightest stoop, alarmingly noticeable to Saffi, if not to him. Take me with you, she had pleaded. Things went wrong all around her and she was helpless to prevent it. She yearned for a normal life, like other girls her age. Couldn't her daddy see that? She beat her fists against his chest and he caught her hands in his, still muscular, fit, in spite of the injury to his back, and he said, "Hold on there, little girl, that's enough of that." Saffi swore she'd never speak to him again if he left and he said, "Well, Sugar, if that's how you feel." But she did speak to him. She kept in touch. Several years later, in Ontario, he got married for a second time, to someone called Liz, and then in the nineteen-eighties he went back to school and became a photocopier repairperson.

"What did you say your job was again?" Saffi would tease him on the phone. "Could you repeat that? Could you just run that by me again?" She made him laugh. He said she must have inherited his sick sense of humour.

"Daddy," she said. "I wish I could see you. I really miss you."

He mumbled something and then recovered and said, in his new brusque yet genial voice, the voice of a man in business, with business contacts and a little windowless office of his own, that she would always be his girl. Of course she would.

"I know that," she said. "I know."

But the summer she was seven, a little girl in a sundress, her hair in pigtails, she didn't believe anything could change in her life. She wouldn't allow it. "I am not moving to a new house," she said, kicking at the table legs. She sat there crayoning the pictures in her colouring book black and purple. She gave the sun a mad face. Outside there was Arthur Daisy's house with a cellar like a dungeon and a bird-boy trapped in it. He had claws and a head full of feathers. If she stayed close nothing bad would come to him, nothing bad; he would sleep and wake and sleep again and one day he'd fly up into the air, blinking at the light. Shoo, she'd say to him, and he'd fly off like a ladybug.

July 1964. There were dogs at the old potato farm, straining at their leashes, anxious to be let go, to pick up a scent and run with it along the banks of the Millstone River. Or who knows, maybe the dogs dreamed of steak dinners and only pretended to sniff the ground. Whatever it was, they didn't seem to have much luck.

It was a day of brilliant sun eclipsed at intervals by dark, scudding clouds. And there was Arthur Dawsley, a man in his late sixties, a bachelor or perhaps a widower, a man seemingly without family of his own, a volunteer member of the search party, after all, in spite of his age. He was given a clipboard and a pencil and told to keep track of the other volunteers. At the end of the day his shoulders drooped a little with fatigue. He wasn't much help, really, more of a diversion, chatting to the police officers, reminiscing about a time when you didn't have to lock your doors at night, you could forget your wallet in a public place and pick it up later, the bills still folded inside, those were the words people used, the bills still folded neatly inside, meaning it no doubt as an affirmation of some kind, nostalgia for a vanished code of ethics or morality; wishful thinking.

Arthur Dawsley was a likeable old guy, or maybe not so likeable, maybe more of a nuisance, full of questions and bright ideas, not that they were of any real value. Not everyone appreciated him. A young cop by the name of Alex Walters gave him a hollow, exasperated stare and for a moment wanted to ask him why he was so darned curious and where he'd been, exactly, on the afternoon young Eugene Dexter was last seen, wearing a blue cotton jacket and carrying two new Marvel comics, the jacket and the comics—or was it a catcher's mitt?—discovered at the bottom of this field, or was it at the end of the road in a ditch, he'd have to check the report again to be sure. It was just a fleeting thought that came to him, a result of his increasing sense of fatigue and irritation, more than anything, although for a moment the thought felt right, felt germane, almost woke him up, then got pushed to the back of his mind.

What kind of a boy had he been? What kind of boy, before he was lost forever? It was said he was in the habit of wandering around on his own and that he had a passion for collecting butterflies and tadpoles, that he'd been a good student who had, at the assembly on the last day of school, received an award for academic achievement and a trophy for sportsmanship, his name inscribed for posterity on a little silver plaque. He was well-liked, mischievous, yet thoughtful, a little withdrawn at times, unexpectedly serious, old for his years, some said. For weeks, for months, there had been posters stapled to telephone poles, pictures of the missing boy, his hair sticking up a little in front, a wide smile, his teeth milk-white and slightly protuberant, a small dimple at the corner of his mouth. An ordinary boy. His parents' only son. How was it possible that he was there one day and gone the next? And how was it possible that not one but two boys had vanished within a few weeks of each other, as if they'd never existed, or as if they had existed merely to be each other's shadow image, a sad confirmation.

There were no answers, it seemed. It was a genuine mystery that infected the town like a virus and then suddenly cleared up, leaving as an after-effect an epidemic of amnesia. Not even the land appeared to remember: each spring the old potato farm erupted in a vigorous new crop of tufted grasses and coarse-leafed weeds drenched in dew, lop-sided with spit-bug saliva. Tiny grey moths and butterflies patterned like curtains rose up in clouds. Birds nested in the trees. Children played there, running through the long grass, switching each other across the shins with willow branches. On the other side of the Millstone River the marsh got set aside as a park and bird sanctuary and Saffi walked there almost every day when her own children were young and even she didn't always remember. The field she glimpsed on the far side of the river did not seem like the same field. That was, it did and did not look the same. For one thing, the town had grown up around it, crowding at its outermost boundaries. Some of the alders and hawthorns near the river had been cut down. But it remained just a field, innocent, mild, apart.

For each separate person the Earth came into being. It began its existence anew and surprised everyone with its beauty. So Saffi believed. The loss of any individual, any single life, must, therefore, dull the perception of beauty. Wasn't that true? Loss was something you fought against. But if it happened you got over it, because what choice did you have? You recovered and went on. Wasn't that what the therapists meant, when they used the word "healing?" Wasn't that the promise implicit in therapy, and, for that matter, in religion? *And all the fine maidens will not go to clay!*

What did Saffi know? What had she seen and forgotten, or not forgotten, but remembered, shakily, in fragments that, once re-assembled, would make up a picture she could scarcely bear to contemplate? For a time she'd suffered with some kind of anxiety disorder, quite incapacitating and disagreeable. She no longer took medication; she had no need of it. But what a struggle at times! And it was difficult to pinpoint a cause for the spells of depression and exhaustion and what she could only think of as an unnameable dread, a nearly living presence that did, at times, choose to haunt her. She'd gone through a difficult time when she was first married, when the children were babies, but she'd recovered, hadn't she? She just didn't have the luxury of understanding every little thing that had happened in her life. How many people did? Memory was so imperfect. The habit of reticence, of keeping secrets was, on the other hand, easily perfected; it was powerful and compelling, irresistible.

She was a vigilant parent. She couldn't help it. If she lost sight of her kids, even for the briefest space of time, she felt a bleak, enervating moment of inevitability and it was as if she herself had vanished, as if the world was simply gone, all its substance and splendour disintegrating into nothing, but she wouldn't allow it; she wouldn't. Just as her Aunt Loretta had taught her to love and respect nature, to study and give names to all things, trees, grasses, wildflowers, all growing things, Saffi passed on to her children what she laughingly called *my arcane secrets*. Because wasn't there something arcane and essentially troubling in wild plants, their brief tenure on Earth and straggling indiscriminate growth, their contradictory natures, both healing and destructive, the small stink of death like a reproach or accusation at the heart of each intricately devised and not always beautiful flower? Not always so beautiful.

She taught her children to be observant, to see the architectural wonder of an ant's nest glistening like molten lava in the sun. Listen to the crickets, she said. Look at the mallard ducks, how they swim in pairs, peaceably, male and female. Look at the dragonflies, filled with light, primitive, unsteady, like ancient aircraft. Even: Look at this robin's egg, shattered, vacant, useless. Look at this dead raccoon, its paws stiff as hooks. Go ahead, look, she said. It won't hurt you to look.

She had a recurring dream, only it was more the memory of a dream that recurred, rather than the dream itself. In the dream she got up from her bed and went outside. She could hear a sound that filled the air all around and when she crawled through the hedge and came out the other side like something being born into night she could see Arthur Daisy by his shed, the door swinging open. Inside the shed it seemed there was a greater darkness than the moonless dark of night. There was Arthur Daisy, striking with his shovel at the ground, baked hard as clay after a long drought interrupted only by that one downpour the day the search party went out with the dogs and all the other useless things they took, sticks to beat down the grass and maps and walkie-talkie radios. All of them searching in the wrong place. Saffi was the only one who knew. But who would listen to her? *What was true and what was something else, a made-up story?*

It happened on the seventh day of the seventh month; Saffi was seven years old. She saw the sevens in a line, affronted, braced like sailors, their little tongues of flame licking at the air. They linked up and made a barbed-wire fence no-one could get through. They made a prison-house no-one could enter.

A mist was rising over the yard. In the mist was a turtle-dove. The bird-boy wasn't lost anymore. He wasn't a boy waiting near a riverbank for a shape to appear dark and comic and dangerous as a troll. He was indeed a turtledove, soaring higher and higher, giving the night a sort of radiance that came from within, his soul or spirit shining out. In the dream Saffi spoke to herself kindly, saying Hush, hush, it's all right, it will be all right, and the only sound that came to her from the soundless well of her dream was the ringing of a shovel against the unyielding earth, at times illusory as a whisk against a tympanum and then again peremptory and doleful as a bell far off in the night.

The Irish Book of Beasts

Bernice Friesen

The following is an excerpt from a novel in progress, The Irish Book of Beasts. *The main character, twelve-year-old James, is about to arrive at his new public school in Cork City, Ireland.*

St. Paul's School was a square of grey stone and blood-brick walls, gravel courtyards and a thick-grassed playing field. The east side edged on a street of middle-class townhouses and a corner grocer's, a street that led down to the centre of Cork City. The North edge of the school grounds ran along College Road near University College and the west edge jutted into an area of mansions. St. Mary's, the girl's convent school, was further south, up the hill. Each school was rich enough to have its own large chapel, each sex entirely cloistered, ignorant, supposedly safe.

St. Paul's was devoted to tradition, the walls serving to keep boys in but also to keep foreign ideas out, even when these new and dangerous ideas came from the Pope himself. The trend to move chapel sanctuaries to central positions of the church in order to better include the congregation was ignored; the sanctuary stayed firmly at the far Eastern end of the cruciform chapel. The boys' showers remained without hot water. On Fridays, fish was served with potatoes and cabbage, not potatoes and carrots, not rice and cabbage.

A private "public" school, it was built after the turn of the century by the country's few wealthy Catholic families, donations from abroad and Church money. There was room for 70 paying residents, 100-odd day boys, and five year-round orphan boys, these charity positions ensured with specific instructions that accompanied an anonymous endowment. The school couldn't claim historic venerability, so the first Jesuit Headmaster, Father Townley, saw to a great planting of ivy, Chinese wisteria, roses and Virginia creeper around every public facing wall and building, twentieth-century brick gradually growing woolly with the green-bearded foliage of respectability.

In the nineteen-twenties, having discovered a passion for fruit and for bending the limbs of trees (as well as boys) to his will, Father Townley brought a small pear cutting from his long dead parents' home in Cornwall, and planted it beside the still barren inner wall of the courtyard, training the growing branches along the brick with wire. It thrived for the next two years, partly because of his promise of a fate worse than death for any boy who so much as spat near it. Every year thereafter, Father Townley bought more and more seedlings: fig, peach, nectarine, quince, Hedelfingen cherry, European and Manchurian apricot, Golden Russet apple, Japanese, European and Fellenberg plum—and pears. He fell in love with pears, their lush, shapely blond fruit. "My Ladies," he called them, the fruit of medieval lasciviousness, the fruit believed to mimic the shape of the female body: Bosc, Beurre d'Anjou, Williams' Bon Chrètien, Flemish Beauty. He studied the art of espalier, slanting his pears and quinces up the walls in straight cordons, bending his apples, plums, cherries, apricots, nectarines and peaches into wondrous fans and lattices against the brick, letting his fig trees grow wild in the corners, and still running the school with an impeccable authority twisted now and then with bright twigs of humour.

Picked by the masters and the orphan boys, Townley's amply rewarded "Fruit Slaves," the Townley fruit graced the tables of the masters every summer, was baked into pies, preserved in Mason jars, and a special basket was always carried by Father Townley himself, in a tiny battered Austin, to the Archbishop of Armagh every August on St. Oswald's day. It was this unceasing devotion with fruit that made an Archbishop, (no-one can remember which) grant Father Townley his only wish: that he should be allowed, upon retirement, to remain at the school to tend his trees. The year Father Townley turned 75, he moved his living quarters from the Headmaster's suite to a tiny room overlooking the courtyard. He took a short vacation to England, returned, and waited for a shipment of 35 peach, apple and of course, pear trees, his first love, to arrive by ship at Cobh. He planted them all in a single day before lying down to rest for two, the first of the young masters coming out to help him at nine in the morning, the second at eleven, and by one in the afternoon, all classes were dismissed, and the masters along the wall with shovels and chicken wire and dirty hands as the boys played a huge rule-less game of soccer in the field, with ten balls and almost 200 players.

Father Townley settled into his life of tending trees, concentrating as he never could before on fighting the brute-named fruit diseases that had plagued him for years—hard wicked names of brown rot, leaf curl, black knot, fire blight, crown rot—cutting out diseased wood, then dunging the roots from an old wooden wheelbarrow some boys had never seen him without. Remarkably, all but two of the saplings survived and Townley trained them in candelabra shapes, free-form flames, a white and pink heat of blossoms against the red brick. They began bearing bushels of fruit within a few years, more than the masters, the orphan boys and the Archbishop of Armagh could pick and eat and preserve at the height of the season. After harvesting as much as they could, the masters opened the doors of the school to the poor, who carried away the apples and pears in potato sacks, in their pockets, in their hands. And still, there was more. Father Townley—already 82, wizened to the size of a twelve-year-old boy, which made his nose and ears appear gargantuan—Father Townley, became a fruit vendor. He hired a donkey cart and a man to take himself, boxes of his fruit and two or three overworked orphan Fruit Slaves, to the Saturday market. From 7 AM to 7 PM, Townley sat beneath an umbrella in his soiled, leaf-smudged, black cassock, watching his boys put pears in the baskets of housewives, squinting and grinning with a mouth containing only one tooth.

He got more and more decrepit as years went by, as boys came and left and the youngest masters aged. Eventually, there was no-one alive who could remember what he had looked like as a man of 40, and his care of the trees began to suffer. He could no longer reach the top branches to prune their wild summer growth. He could no longer distinguish dead and rotting branches from healthy ones. He prowled the grounds of the school with his pruning shears and wheelbarrow, flakes of skin falling from his almost hairless brown-spotted scalp, decaying visibly, moment by moment, an object of terror to the youngest boys.

It was Father Townley who James first met as he entered the gates of the courtyard after walking the three blocks from the bus stop on the main road into Cork City. The old Jesuit had seen him through the wrought iron and waited in ambush for this new one who didn't yet know the rules. He stepped out from behind the wall and seized James by the lapels.

"A fate worse than death," he hissed into James' face, along with the smell of age and the sweet breath of pear juice. These words were thought to be the only ones the old man could remember from the English language.

James screamed, leaped out of the man's feeble grasp, and looked for a way of escape, the gate having swung shut behind him. He saw a tall priest standing at the top of a stairway, a Father Foley from Sligo, at 33, the youngest Jesuit on staff.

"Is that James Young? *Young* James Young who was supposed to arrive on the half-one from Skibbereen? Welcome. And I see ye've already introduced yourself to the most respected resident of the school."

The next afternoon, hidden on the top of the maintenance shed roof, James and his new roommates watched as old Father Townley began attacking a Virginia creeper with sailors curses and a kitchen knife because it was creeping too close to one of his Flemish Beauties. Two of the masters talked the knife out of his hand and gently led him away to the hospital. He died that night, from a brain haemorrhage, three days before his ninety-seventh birthday. There were many local people, particularly among his market friends, who believed he died of distress at being separated from his trees. Some said he was older than 97—a hundred and nine—and some said he was a saint, that his body wouldn't decay, that within the gleaming mahogany of the coffin, wasn't the shrivelling worm of death, but a body growing more beautiful, smelling of apples.

The school would never recover from its first headmaster, either his life or his death, and this was made manifest in the homage paid to his trees. Over the previous 50 years, every master starting at Saint Paul's, had been taught the rule of the trees. No-one was allowed to touch them. No-one was allowed to let a hurling ball knock against them or tamper with the wire mesh than protected them from such unfortunate accidents. The masters all came to think of the trees as their ladies, the lost and precious things that represented everything they had given up on taking vows of chastity, on separating themselves from worldly feminine beauty. As they heard Townley himself threaten boys, so they also threatened them with the fate worse than death, a punishment no-one had yet given or explained, a punishment forever lost in Townley's mind.

On the afternoon of the funeral, meant for mourning, James climbed the ladder of Townley's first pear tree, the almost sacred Flemish Beauty, the First Lady, grown thick and doddering on the wall opposite the main gate. The masters were in their study, a dark room of wood and shelves and books and the heavy knocking of an old wall clock. They were observing solemn silence together. Father Foley, always the restless one, looked out the window and screamed. It was a Celtic war-cry he'd acquired genetically through long lines of pure Hybernian blood. Its shattering power nearly caused several more fatalities in the hearts of the older Jesuits who were so startled out of solemn silence, they screamed, too. The Masters charged into the courtyard, hurling outraged fists at James, who lost his balance and fell, grappling for handholds, bringing one core-rotten branch to the ground with him.

James lay at the bottom of a black well of cassocks, silenced by shock and the pain of a broken arm. The masters were at a loss. This was a new boy who obviously hadn't been taught the rules, not with everyone preoccupied with the death and the funeral. There had been minor incidents before, with broken branches, but no-one had ever been caught, and no-one had dared touch the First Lady. No-one had ever encountered the Fate Worse Than Death. If James wasn't made an example of, given something far worse than an ordinary beating, the threat would be seen as hollow, and boys would climb the trees constantly, destroying them. And if the Masters did happen to think up a fate worse than death, how could they explain it to the parents? Meting out a fate worse than death was politically impossible. And how could they strap a boy who was already badly injured? Those ignorant of God's Law are without guilt. Hadn't he already given himself punishment enough?

The older ones walked away to council together, clicking their tongues, aghast, musing on how fortunate it was that Townley himself hadn't lived to see this day. Father Foley took James to the hospital in the Headmaster's Austin, observing the boy with quiet pity, wondering about his fate. The boys who had seen his fall wondered, too, and word of his daring escapade spread through their ranks until even the oldest knew his name, whispered about him with gasps and shaking heads. James, like many condemned criminals, rose to the stature of a folk hero, and he did it in absentia, in less than the space of an hour.

After the plaster had set, Father Foley brought James directly to the dark cherry-wood master's study. The masters had made a decision. The more reasonable brothers had prevailed over those more traditional, who favoured sound beatings for every infraction and demanded James receive double strokes. Headmaster Father Dunnigan put a cold hand on his shoulder.

"I don't think...you realize...what you have done," he said, halting his hollow tomb of a voice after every phrase. "So I shall tell you."

For the next ten minutes, he expounded upon James' hideous crime, and upon the mystery of the punishment no-one had ever been evil enough to deserve—until now. Dunnigan stopped once he thought the desired level of terror had been attained by his small subject. James had turned white, making his freckles stand out like fallen autumn leaves on fine white sand.

"But this...the day the honourable Father Townley was laid to rest...happens to be the only day upon which infractions are required to be forgiven.... It is what he wanted," Dunnigan said, clenching his hands—almost crossing his fingers—during this one little lie. "If you want forgiveness...you may have it.... Do you?"

James nodded: a kind of quiver.

They released him into the hallway and he made his way back to his room, painkillers still fuzzing his brain, silent to the stares of the other boys. He lay on his bed, face to the wall, cradling his plaster cast with his good arm while his roommates stood in an awed little coven outside the door.

"They broke his arm. *Jasus*. He broke a branch so they broke his arm."

The horrified whisper rumoured its way around the whole school, then around Cork City itself, producing a rash of obedience in the boys, and a rash of phone calls from the parents.

An eye for an eye, a tooth for a tooth, and a limb for a limb.

Ex Libris

P.K. Page

PUBLICATION DATE

The book, worked on for years, was finally published the day he was born. It was waiting for him, so to speak, on 3 December. Of course he was too young to read, so his mother read it aloud to him—between feedings. The first snow was falling outside and the household was turned upside down—broken nights and nappies and—a baby! With Christmas looming. Reading it exhausted his poor dear mother and it is unlikely that he understood a word. But it was a major influence in his life, none the less. In fact, it was his life.

His mother read the four-volume edition. It has since been edited, hopefully improved, with certain episodes deleted entirely.

THE EDITED VERSION

I was born into a literate family, literate but far from wealthy —or so I thought. Why have I used "but" where I might have used "and?" As if wealth and literacy are opposed—as indeed they are, today. But surely not then. Many of my parents' friends were layabouts—bookish and broke—so that may be where the idea came from. Today a so-called education prepares you for commerce, not scholarship.

My parents were such avid readers it surprises me that I was conceived at all. I don't quite understand that "at all." Except that it must have been nip and tuck—between the end of *War and Peace* and the start of *The Brothers Karamazov*, perhaps. I think I belonged to the Russian period. It would account for my name.

I WAS AN ONLY, LONELY CHILD.

Oh, they loved me, I feel sure. But it was a literary love—nursery rhymes and Beatrix Potter, fairytales and King Arthur. I liked *Mrs. Tiggy Winkle* and *The Tale of Two Bad Mice*. I also liked Merlin a lot. Dreamed I was the young Arthur. Looked for an excalibur in every stone, thought there might be miniature excaliburs no bigger than darning needles waiting for the bright-eyed. How I polished my eyes! And I longed to be the youngest son in those fairytales where three brothers set out to win the treasure. I suppose I *was* the youngest, but as I was also the oldest and the middle one as well it seemed to cancel me out.

They didn't converse much, my parents—even with each other. "Brilliant!" my mother would say, handing a hardcover to my father who would give her a metallic glance through his reading glasses. That was about all that passed between them. And the books kept piling up. Everywhere. In my tiny bedroom a narrow path between stacks of books—read and unread—lead to my cot. My nightmares—I was a fire child, and the least fever induced hallucinations—usually consisted of two people building a wall of books higher and higher. No room for windows or doors. No room for the light. Just little me in my sleepers tossing on my cot in a paper canyon.

BUT IT WAS NOT A NARROW LIFE.

I defy anyone to contradict me. What most people didn't know was that I was given to out-of-body experiences. Or, out of *my* body and into that of a dog. Always a dog. Sometimes rough-haired, sometimes smooth-haired. I can still feel the collar of rough hair, the taste of a leather leash. The sleekness of hair as smooth as skin. Even today I cannot see a dog—any dog—without feeling my being enter into its being, rejoice in its being. Feel the difference in the blood—the astonishing difference in the blood. Don't think dogs don't think—you, who have never been one. Take my word for it. They do.

Serious long thoughts about bones. A flutter of thoughts about running and jumping and the most extraordinary thoughts about smells—near-epiphanies.

You might have expected me to react against this life of books and parents and dogs' bodies and seek out other kids, tough ones maybe, or at least, jocks. But I suppose genes play a large part, especially before experience has entered the picture. I was pretty much the cat that walked by itself. But there were kids, occasionally. One little girl on our street took down her underpants in her dad's garage and I stared in a kind of bewilderment at her malformation. Thought about it a lot, actually. A sort of pink wall. It stays in my mind mixed with the smell of engine oil. Other than that my world was mainly books, just as my parents' was. I believe I was precocious. Used words like "fenestration" and "lazareto" and "recanalization." I liked to see the look on people's faces.

I don't remember being unhappy, beyond having spots. All the other manifestations of puberty and adolescence were dealt with adequately by my father. He was intelligent. And scientific in a way for all his love of literature.

At college I lived in the stacks.

Where else? They were just like my bedroom, but organized. Besides, I was bred for stacks. Long legs, long arms. Good eyes that I had polished. I began by reading the As. It took me a long time to get to Auden. You can imagine. Even with *my* eyes. But when I did, I fell in love. At home I had been immersed in the classics. I knew my Shakespeare and I loved him, even tolerated wordy old Wordsworth. My parents were into modern translations of all kinds—Rilke, Lorca, Seferis. Although translations intrigued me, I wanted the real thing. Auden was it. He was like jazz. I devoured him. Funny, really, because he was dead, for pete's sake. Long dead.

There are people on earth who are dead and don't know it. Walk-

ing about. I read it in a book. Are the dead—Auden, for instance—those who have returned, believing themselves still alive? Slow learners, you might say. Or are they the living—my Mum and Dad? Me? It makes me uneasy. How can I prove to myself I am living?

> Dead: having the appearance of death; lacking power to move, feel, or respond; very tired; incapable of being stirred emotionally or intellectually; grown cold; no longer producing or functioning; no longer having interest, relevance or significance.

What if I answer "yes" to those definitions—am I dead, then? Dead before achieving anything. Unlike Auden. Alack, alas. Alas, alack.

BUT BLESS MY LONG ARMS AND LEGS.

I was made for basketball. My game drove spectators wild. In a team I moved slow motion, or so it appeared. People who watched said they were caught in two time streams. It affected the circuits in their brains.

Ivor moves like slow honey. All the other guys are like bees.

I didn't know what they meant. I was just playing the game. But as they liked it, I was happy for them. At first I had played unselfconsciously. Then the shouts of the crowd reached me and I began to love those shouts. Soon I played for the shouts alone. Became aware of every move I made. It wasn't that I was actually slow but my long arms and legs made me look slow. I took one step where others took two or three. Then I developed a taste for slowness and began to test just how slowly I could pass and run without actually stopping. A slow dribble drove the crowd mad. It was as if all the clocks had run down, they told me. Dreamy. For me *and* the spectators. Our team was a sensation. We won every game.

We were national champions when a scout got to me and I found myself on an all-black team. The Tall Boys. We matched, The Tall Boys and I. Arms and legs long. Polished eyes. There was no difference in our timing. We were all slow honey. But I was the only white. It was the first time such a thing had happened in the annals of the sport. I was called "nigger-lover," I was called "piss-ass." But the crowd loved me and we took all the games. Slow and dreamy. Even my parents raised their eyes from their books and looked at me with surprise. Between *War and Peace* and *The Brothers...* they had conceived a star.

The year we took the world I married Esmeralda.

MY BLACK ORCHID, I CALLED HER.

A cliché, I know. Long arms and long legs. Eyes polished. Like me. Black and white, white and black, our languorous, violent love. Nothing had prepared me for Esmeralda. To love her was my career. I embraced it. My body, her body—I no longer knew which was which. I loved her as I loved myself.

I am not proud of this blatant declaration of self-love. It makes me uneasy. *We love ourselves first, our friends second, God last. It should be the reverse.* Where had I read *that*? Interesting that friends remain in the middle, either way. If I were to say, I loved myself as I loved Esmeralda, would anything change? The idea is provocative. And let me provoke myself further, blaspheme, perhaps: I loved her as I love God.

An observant reader will notice the tenses: I loved her as I love God. Do I not love her still? I do.

BUT I CANNOT GO INTO THAT YET.

I was wealthy, of course. I had amassed a fortune. Basketball became a thing of the past. I didn't even watch the games. I

112

might have coached, I suppose, and without Esmeralda, I probably would have. But with Esmeralda there, in my arms as I wakened—long arms, long legs—what choice did I have? We made love. It was my vocation; my avocation.

On Sundays we went to her church and sang. Holy Saints. She was another Kathleen Battle. And the whole congregation sang too. Lordy! Lordy! There had been nothing like that in my literary childhood. Nothing like that at all. No room for music among all the words. And now I was swamped by it, overwhelmed, in fact. What was this art that demanded your entire lung power—took your breath and gave it back, took your breath and gave it back. It was more like a kind of sport. Writing, painting, sculpture required no special breathing. Only dance. And music. My voice came out of some hidden vault. "They crucified my Lord."

I WENT TO SEE MY PARENTS FROM TIME TO TIME.

Their world didn't change. They had neither computer nor TV. The house was solid with books—a book meatloaf. They couldn't bring themselves to get rid of any of them. Easier they said, to get rid of furniture. They sold the chesterfield, all but two armchairs, and the spare bed. As a concession to me, they read Tony Morrison. Living through books, as they did, with no time for life, nothing had readied them for *Beloved*. Surely, I thought, in all that reading, they would have learned something about racism. But, "White people don't behave like that," they said, a questioning tone in their voices, as if asking me to agree. I replied that white people do. All people do. We are half animal and half angel. A very difficult mix. They could only shake their heads—my father's, now, a shock of grey, my mother's turning white at the temples. They were old.

AS FOR ME....

I was putting on weight—thickening through the waist. Even

my once so muscular thighs were becoming flabby.

One morning Esmeralda wakened, and instead of turning to me lazy and drowsy as usual, she sprang out of bed and turned on the shower. The scent of her gel, heavy as gardenias, filled the air. Oh, Proust, do I not know what you mean? That smell would come to conjure up my whole life with Esmeralda.

"What's up?" I asked, unbelieving.

"I've got a job," she said. "Modelling."

"Modelling! A job! What the heck? We don't need the money, honey."

"Somebody in this family's got to work. It's only right."

The logic of it was absurd. I saw, in a flash, that I didn't know Esmeralda—how her mind worked, what her thoughts were. It was terrifying. I went into the bathroom and pulled her beautiful black naked body to me. "Honey," I said. "Don't leave me. We've got to get to know each other."

"No talk of leaving," Esmeralda said. "I just need to find myself. I don't want to be a sex object all my life."

A sex object! Esmeralda? "You are my love, my life," I said. There were tears in my eyes.

"*Yours*," she said. "That's the whole point."

IF I WERE TO TELL YOU MY WORLD FELL APART....

It did. Morning to night, my life was a vacuum. Her hatbox, her cosmetic case, her beautiful long arms and legs, her polished eyes. She had no place left in her heady, hectic life for her lover. With those looks, with that voice, she was destined for stardom and she knew it. Something any fool could see.

And now I was any fool. Every fool. Why had I not seen it before?

I took to pacing back and forth like an Alzheimer's patient. As if the very action of my feet could heal my heart. I saw Esmeralda less and less. Photo shoots, fashion shows, beauty parlours. New York, Paris, Rome, Singapore. She bought a pale Afghan hound—her perfect match, even as I had been—who walked at the end of a golden leash. They modelled together. Sometimes she phoned, sometimes she was too busy. Lonely, I sought her on TV. She was on shampoo ads—her long shiny black hair lifted by a fan. Tampons, pantyhose, face cream. Sometimes because of the lighting, the camera angle, the hairdo, I barely knew her. Recognized her just as the image faded, and my heart broke.

I spent more and more time in front of TV. Took to drinking beer. Alone.

When she came home with the dog after months abroad, I was waiting for her, avid for her. And the dog. I had begun to see the dog as me—or me as the dog. Which? Those long legs, that pale fur. I wondered if that was why she bought it.

She was astonishing. I could hardly believe her. Always dazzling, she was now perfect, with the dog on a long golden leash. I wanted to fling my arms around her but as soon as my eyes fell on the dog I had an out-of-body experience.

I was that dog. And hostile. I strained at the leash. "Heel, Holly, heel," she said firmly, and yanked my collar. It was a choke-leash and she almost strangled me. "This is Ivor. Nice Ivor," she said, and patted me. But Holly hated "nice Ivor" and lunged again. *And I was Holly. Holly was me.*

It lasted no longer than a minute or so. I don't think Esmeralda even noticed but it unnerved me. Of all the dogs I had ever been, I had never been a dog that disliked me.

"He usually loves people," Esmeralda said and I felt accusation in her tone. Then her eyes looked me over. My thick waistline had become a paunch. It was not disguised by the new Armani jacket I had bought especially for her. With my unmanicured hands I reached out to her. "Don't touch me!" she said in a sharp voice I had not heard her use before. And Holly lunged again.

IN SHORT, HER HOMECOMING WAS A DISASTER.

We never made love. That dog wouldn't let us. And the telephone, the fax machine, the e-mails all interfered. A steady stream of beauticians came to the house. She worked out.

"I have to tell you," she said, between appointments, "I'm leaving for Hollywood."

"Hollywood!"

"Yep. I'm going to play Josephine Baker. They tell me I'm made for it."

"Josephine Baker!" I could only repeat what she said. I had no words of my own, apparently. "Josephine Baker," I said again.

"The great jazz singer!" She was impatient.

"Can you sing jazz?"

"I can sing anything, honey. Just you watch."

I didn't know this Esmeralda. I had never seen this confident metallic woman in my life before. Where had she come from? "Esmeralda..." I pleaded. But she was on the phone again and that goddam dog was between us, always between us. A canine wall.

BEFORE I KNEW IT SHE HAD GONE.

I looked at the desolation of the house. Garment bags, tissue paper, cardboard boxes. Our bathroom full of lotions and creams and gels. There was barely room for my razor.

WHEN THE TELEPHONE RANG I DIDN'T ANSWER.

I was not going to be her appointments secretary. Let it ring. She isn't here. Let it go on ringing. But the persistent bell in the empty house was intolerable. Just to shut it up, I lifted the receiver. It was my father's voice.

"Ivor, I've been trying to reach you? Your mother is dying."

My head was so full of Esmeralda I couldn't take it in.

"Ivor, did you hear me?"

"Mum?" I said. Mum couldn't die. He must be wrong.

"She had a stroke and they say.... Oh, son, can you not come home?"

AND SO I WENT.

Threw my razor into a bag along with my pyjamas and a change of shirt and shorts and caught the first plane out.

I hardly knew my father. He was a stick of skin. Small, grey, broken. He led me through walls of books, up the dusty stairs and into their bedroom. There was barely room for both of us beside the bed. My mother lay, her right side paralyzed. Her face twisted. Unrecognizable. But on the floor beside her bed, open and face down, as if she had put it there before turning off the light, lay Emily Dickinson's poems.

"She wouldn't have been able to read," I said, looking at the book and then at her.

"What? What's that you said?" Perhaps my father was deaf.

"Left hemisphere," I continued, not believing my words, my mother, the crypt of books we stood in.

"Speak to her, son," my father said.

I didn't know what to say. Then, "It's Ivor, Mum. Ivor." My voice sounded like a kid's.

"Mum. Mum!" Her left eyelid flickered. "Oh, Mum!" But her face closed again into that contorted mask.

I thought my chest would break. I had to get out of there. I pushed past my father, past all those piles of books, looking for a place to sit down. The house smelled like an antiquarian bookstore. At last, in the kitchen, I found a chair. My chest broke. I began to sob. I sobbed for my mother, for my father, for Esmeralda. And I sobbed for myself.

OH, I LOOKED AFTER WHAT HAD TO BE DONE.

Hired a nurse. Cleared a wider passageway to the bedroom between the books. Got some order in the kitchen. Bought some eggs. And settled in to wait. There is a lot of waiting in a house of death. A lot of standing, hands hanging helpless. Useless rearranging of sheets and pillows. "A little jelly, Mum?" "Some mango ice cream?"

I had picked up the Emily Dickinson beside her bed and now I opened it. It had been read and re-read, marked in pencil with stars, asterisks, underlinings. Poems about Death.

Because I could not stop for Death
He kindly stopped for me.

Did she suspect, in her pell-mell race through literature, that He was about to stop? Probably not. More likely it was the poetry she loved. The turn of phrase. Dickinson's unique turn of phrase.

When I began basketball I forgot books. Really didn't miss them. And then Esmeralda wiped my tapes completely. Now, suddenly, I longed for literature. A spring of fresh water gushed as I read. Plants bloomed. I read hungrily.

> The manner of the Children—
> Who weary of the Day—
> Themself—the weary Plaything
> They cannot put away—

How did she know all that—that spinster Emily in her white house behind white curtains? How could she possibly know what I felt? A weary Plaything. Weary to death.

I was astonished by my grief. This old lady who had conceived me between books, given birth to me between books and read to me, sometimes at great cost to herself, would read to me no more. But as her farewell present she gave me Emily Dickinson.

MY FATHER AND I WERE THE ONLY MOURNERS.

My father a little stick figure clutching a bunch of summer flowers. Delphiniums, daisies, roses—yellow and pink.

We returned, drained, from the crematorium to that comfortless warehouse he called home. With the nurse gone, my mother gone, the place was dust and debris. We hardly spoke, my father and I. I poured us a whisky. Later, I scrambled us some eggs. Then we crashed.

What to do now? I thought, as I wakened. The books towered above and around me, stacked helter-skelter. I heard my father moving about downstairs. I thought of Esmeralda, beautiful Esmeralda in Hollywood with that goddam dog. And I wondered where I—the star, the guy with the beautiful wife—had vanished to? The whole tone of my life had altered. No longer a figure to be envied, I was a deserted husband with a father bereft, in a house of despair. Psychologists have a name for it: mid-life crisis, they call it. Damn them.

THEN MY FATHER DIED.

I found myself the sole inheritor of a surprising amount of money, an old house in a run-down neighbourhood, and thousands of books. My first thought was to call in a second-hand bookseller and get rid of them all. But I moved slowly, hobbled by inertia. Esmeralda's absence, the death of both parents—the enormity of my inheritance....

But little by little, book by book, I got sucked into that dust-filled vortex. A most eclectic library—if a jumble could be graced by such a name. I was interested to see that the largest single category was poetry. Art books were perhaps second—the surrealists from Bosch to Ernst and Carrington—and the whole history of art. Folktales, science fiction: Verne and H.G. Wells and Abbott's *Flatland* as well as Clarke and Sturgeon and the inner space fiction of Lessing, plus people I had never heard of. Their astonishing thoughts about time and space turned me upside down. The literature of ideas. I had read nothing like it in contemporary fiction—a genre noticeably absent in my parents' collection, as far as I could see. "If you don't read the bestsellers when they first come out," my father had said, "you don't need to read them at all." Perhaps he was right.

Had my parents absorbed this wealth of ideas, I wondered? And if so, what did it profit them? Why had I not spent more time at home, asking them questions, instead of goofing off with Esmeralda? But that was what I thought with Esmeralda *gone*. What would I have thought if she had suddenly appeared?

DID I SAY I LOVED HER?

I do.

BOOKS, BOOKS, BOOKS.

They became my life, even as they had been my parents' life. Lethargy and inertia were things of the past. I was on fire.

I found an unemployed librarian and together we began the interminable work of sorting and cataloguing. I installed a computer and the software required for itemizing what, at times, felt like the contents of the city dump. We wore masks against the dust of decades. We found treasures and learned skills I could not have dreamed of. And although, originally, I thought we should construct a special building for the books, I soon discovered that the house was well enough built for us to renovate. So I hired carpenters and designers. Shelves rose in all the rooms. Floors were reinforced. Temperature and humidity controls installed.

When not working on the project, I was reading. I became a vessel for all that print to pour into. And the hallucination of my childhood—of book building upon book and blocking the light—was now reversed, and book building upon book was letting the light *in*. I had had no idea how many combinations and computations of words there were, no idea of the extent of human thought—psychological, philosophical, spiritual. I began to sense space/time, stretching back to the beginnings of language and beyond, and forward beyond my imagination's reach. The world that had seemed large enough to me when I had Esmeralda—a bed-sized world—was now, without her, immense. A vast glass-house, light-filled. A night sky by day, if one can conceive of such a thing.

I had calls from her occasionally. The filming was going well. She was "a natural," they told her. Everyone loved Holly. And what did I think about a divorce?

And then it came to me. A vast glass-house was exactly what I wanted—an atrium with a glass ceiling—UV glass, of course —around which the books.... How my thoughts raced. The property next door was for sale. I snapped it up. And hired an architect, the best I could find. To hell with the cost. I wanted the space to reflect the contents. A glass bomb.

THE WORK WAS A WONDER.

Even before it was finished—half-finished—librarians and architects beat a path, as they say. The architects were stunned by the cantilevered extension which took in the property next door. And the light pouring in. The librarians didn't quite know why I featured Auden so prominently. Not only did I include his complete works, but all books with references to him—*Evening Light at Sandover,* for example, in which he comes back as a shade, conjured by Merril. And the David Hockney drawing, blown up, life size, of his raddled face—the only face I know with actual runnels in it. I told them I planned to do the same with certain other authors—chosen in a somewhat idiosyncratic manner, or seemingly so. Persian miniatures for Hakim Sanai, perhaps, or elegantly handset, a quotation from him: "The human's progress is that of one who has been given a sealed book written before he was born." The Modigliani drawing of Akmatova for her section, of course. What would I use for Immanuel Velikofsky and his *Worlds in Collision*? Something from an observatory—the heavens blazing. Or I could hire an artist, for pete's sake. Why not? And why Velikofsky, come to that? Was he one of my faves? Actually no. He may have been a nut. But that Immanuel shook things up—questioned all those scientists locked in their certainties. I like doubt cast on conventional wisdom. I guess I like doubt a lot.

The librarians shook their serious heads—this was not according to the book, ha, ha—but they took notes.

MEANWHILE

The neighbourhood altered. Old houses became boutiques and delis. Were remodelled for the wealthy young. What a change-about. And at its centre, at its very heart—the library. It shone.

A PHENOMENON, NOT A FOLLY.

My parents' obsession, now an idiosyncratic collection of paintings and books, was written up in the press, in architectural journals, in librarians' bulletins. It created world-wide attention.

And that attention generated work—more than our small staff could handle. We appointed a Board, a Chairman of the Board—me. We hired experts. And we had an official opening where speeches were made and ribbons cut. There had never been such an event. Artists and writers, bureaucrats of culture—celebrities of all kinds—fought to attend.

Esmeralda swanned in—a creature from another planet. All jewels and line. "Where is Holly?" I asked. Her beautiful eyes swam with tears. "Dead," she said. "Run over." I put my arm around her. "Ivor," she said, "you are like a brother," and for the briefest moment her glittering body relaxed against me. But then she was on stage again, camera men crowding, flash-bulbs popping. And before I knew it she was gone.

DO I STILL LOVE HER?

I do.

I HAD BUILT MY SHINING PALACE.

Out of tears, perhaps. It was dedicated to the memory of my parents, to Emily Dickinson, and W.H. Auden. Their names were engraved on a tablet in the foyer. The foyer that had once been our small book-jammed hall.

The days after the opening were crammed with appointments—the Ministry of Culture, the International Commission on the Arts. No time to read. Once again, no time to read. Exhausted, I dashed from interviews to meetings, from hotels to boardrooms.

BECAUSE I COULD NOT STOP FOR DEATH

I was late for my last appointment of the day—a TV appearance. It was rush hour. I stood on the curb waiting for the light. And then I saw a dog, a terrified dog, running in and out between the cars. In a flash I was out of my body and into that dog.

HE STOOD ON THE CURB WAITING FOR THE LIGHT.

He had no idea he was approaching death. But as he entered the body of the dog, he suddenly remembered what his mother had read him when he lay in her arms—a babe, newborn—tiny, squalling, wanting to be fed.

Comedian Tire

Bill Gaston

Buddhism says there's no beginning nor end to suffering, so in that sense there's no beginning nor end to this story—which is also about how humour lives in the very heart of suffering, and pops up like a neon clown from its big black box.

The background to the story involves my brother Ron, who a year ago at age 50 had a stroke. He survived with huge holes in his memory, dragging a foot, slurring, and utterly pissed off. Apparently strokes at his age aren't so rare. But, though he's ten years older than I am, in the ugly stew of emotions his illness brewed for me, one of the worst was a sense of my own mortality. And then my guilt at that. Watching him limp around in terminal despair, how could I possibly think about myself? But he looks like me. At the root of myself I could trade places.

A month ago it got worse. Ron had a series of heavier strokes, was now truly demolished, dying—could die at any time from a next stroke—and was placed in extended care with elderly people who are similarly bedridden and waiting for death. Ron can no longer walk, talk, control his bowels, eat on his own. I can see he recognizes me, but my arrivals lift his spirits not one bit. Waiting for the final oblivion, he stares at game shows with the other, older residents, unable to ask someone to please turn off this pap and stick in a decent movie. Or whatever. I don't know if he could follow a movie, or if he wants one, but from his eyes I know that he hates what he's watching, the canned laughter blasting the room and its dying, demented, warehoused bodies.

With Ron in Vancouver, and me on the Island, my

monthly planning involves working out when next I can steal two days to ferry over and visit. Kyle's soccer tournaments, our baby daughter Lily, my wife Leslie's work schedule, not to mention my own, plus dentists, doctors, barbecues. All fight my attempts to get over and see Ron, who I don't really want to see, and who maybe doesn't want to see me either. Add to this mix my car—an '89 minivan—which lately has been stalling at intersections. Leslie has demanded a tune-up for some time now, using the words "dangerous" and "Lily" in the same sentence. In my list of things to do, double underlined was the note, *Fix van, visit Ron.*

I'm within walking distance of one of those red and white retail establishments with the red garage bays, and I took it there for that reason. I'd heard general warnings about the place, but in other cities I'd gone there for basic servicing and nothing bad had come of it, aside from being dinged the expected unexpected extras. Lots of cars sat out front waiting to get in, a good sign. The van needed a tune-up is all, and anybody with dirty fingernails can do a tune-up. I asked the man behind the counter for an oil change and tune, and to call me if they found anything big. Maybe I could catch the ferry that night, visit Ron in the morning, then stop by his apartment and load up. That was part of the reason I was avoiding this next visit: Ron would not be going home again and his apartment needed cleaning out. He would no longer in life be needing his clothes, furniture, CDs. My parents were pressing me. Either I come pick up his stuff or they'd "just have to put it out in the street." I didn't want to go and sort through his stuff because then I would have to think about Ron. My connection to Ron.

Ron, you see, is a hard-assed guy. A racist right-winger. We've never agreed on much. We've used our age difference as an easy excuse not to talk. But to put Ron in a nutshell: when I was nine, and he was nineteen, Ron went to the States and enlisted to fight in Vietnam. (Over a thousand Canadians actually did that.) I vaguely recall him talking about "gooks," and remember thinking the whole idea pretty cool as I marched off with my crooked stick to shoot at shadows in the woods behind the house. Though he didn't see action he returned as gook-hating as ever, despite the peace movement in particular and the Age of Aquarius in general.

In the years we both lived at home, I never did get to know him well. I remember closed doors, lots of being ignored, a few bored shoves when I got too close. Years later, smirking, he bought me and my friends our first case of beer. In fairness I'll add that he was never unkind to my mother, and he had the sense to keep quiet about my father's summer in Kelowna. Ron and I communicated with severe, silent eye contact over that one, and I believe that's as intimate as we ever got.

It's been hard to admit to myself that I'm in no hurry to see him again, my own brother. The last time I visited Extended Care it was excruciating to watch him being lifted out of bed for his bath. His eyes were sunken and he'd lost his muscle. They use this wheeled crane that hoists a body up in a canvas sling. An attendant on each arm. Slowly airborne, Ron began to panic, or maybe it was pain—eyes bugging, he whimpered and slobbered and both hands clawed and convulsed minutely. He looked pleadingly to me and all I could do was avoid his eyes and smile a smile so hollow it said that all was fine because now he was going to have his nice bath. Half the horror came out of questions coming at me over the hum of the crane motor: How do I feel for this man who is my brother? What is carried in genes and what does the word "brother" mean? Here is a man I'd avoid if I weren't related to him. He is suffering in ways I can't comprehend and might be better off dead. Do I want him dead? For what reasons, exactly?

The garage place called me late that afternoon, saying they'd indeed found serious problems. As a matter of course they'd conducted their "21-point inspection" and found the van lacked rear brakes, the emergency cable was frozen, and the horn didn't work. The total cost would be $700.

"The stalling," I said. "Did you find the reason for the stalling?" The brakes had been feeling okay to me, and I'd known about the emergency cable, rusted in place by New Brunswick road salt some six years ago. I guess I never used the horn.

"It's stalling?"

"I brought it in because it's stalling. When you stop at a light it idles really—"

"That's your basic tune-up," he said.

"Okay. I just want the tune-up. And an oil change please."

"I really, really wouldn't advise you driving it off the lot with no rear brakes." He paused, during which time I closed my eyes. "I couldn't help noticing your baby seat? It's not my business to say, but—"

"Okay. Forget the horn, forget the emergency cable. Go ahead on the rear brakes."

"Go ahead then?"

"Yes."

He said it would be ready by noon.

That night I was telling Leslie how odd it was, Ron's present situation. At his age so feeble, and him a man who'd always valued, and assumed, his physical strength. He'd worked mainly in heavy equipment (pretending he was driving a tank, I joked to myself), for the last decade building local wharves with a pile-driving outfit. He often had his shirt off, and grease on his considerable chest muscles. He was one of those guys you see yelling to other guys over the roar of machinery, their shoulders glowing bigger than their hardhats.

But what I was describing to Leslie was that virtually all the attendants in extended care were Asian. Here was a man who'd never seen fit to distinguish between Chinese, Japanese, Vietnamese, whomever. They were small, sly, and in his country for no good reason. I'd not heard the word for a while: gooks. And now, bedridden, unable to move or speak, Ron was being tended to by gooks.

I described the scene to Leslie. Ron, already pissed off at his traitorous body, and here's this stream of Asian caregivers—most were Philippino actually—dressing him, sponging his private parts, feeding him his baby food, and keeping up a gay, accented banter: *Okay, Ron! How you do today! Boy, you big! You getting bigger I think!* Talking to him like a child as they stripped or sponged or fed. I found I couldn't begrudge them their lack of sincerity. A job like that, it was amazing that they managed to feign cheer.

128

But the look in Ron's eyes. As if he were assessing a persistent and violently bad dream. I tried to describe it to Leslie. She used the word "karma." I pictured one of Dante's poetic hells.

Ron's situation—his being tended by cheerful, fast-moving Asians—is something I would have liked to ask him about. I tell myself there's lots about Ron I would like to learn, but I wonder if that's because now it's impossible. Another thing I've wanted to ask: did he know what he was doing when he was pretending to shoot gooks? He would fire his air machine gun and make a sound that was exactly "Buddha-Buddha-Buddha-Buddha."

At noon the next day my van sat out on the lot, ready. I entered and announced myself. A long and detailed receipt chugged its way out of the computer. A fellow with "Kyle" on his chest, but no grease under his nails, cheerfully told me I owed $950.

Leslie says I don't stand up for myself. It's true: while not exactly a wimp, I do turn the other cheek. Without going into too much detail here—it's the kind of garage-hell everyone has experienced, after all—I'll just say I did myself proud. First I calmly stated the obvious logic, that since I'd told them to do *less* work than the $700 quote would have paid for, the amount I now owed could not possibly be *more*. Kyle cheerfully said he'd add up the figures again, and did.

"Nope, it's $950," Kyle chirped. He showed me, jabbing his finger on the receipt, how they'd replaced my emergency cable, done my brakes, the horn, lots of labour involved. At the head of the list was the 21-point inspection, for which I was being charged a cute $21.

"I told the guy on the phone to change the oil, tune it and do the rear brakes. That's it. Not the other stuff."

"Well, no sir, you were talking to me, and you said, 'Go ahead.'"

"No I—Well, yeah, go ahead on *the rear brakes*." I jabbed my own finger onto the sheet. "I'm *not* paying for that inspection because I didn't even *want* an inspection, I wanted a *tune-up*." By now a trap door in my gut was swinging open, and I was well into that icy sweat of futility.

"Not what I heard, sir. You said—"

"Even if you *did* all that stuff, it still can't be more than $700. That was the quote. It can't *possibly* be—"

"It was an estimate, sir."

And so on. In the end I loudly threatened (a first for me) to tell my friends about this; I had a lot of friends (a lie) and they all drove shitty cars like mine and used places like this frequently but would no longer. I almost said that I was a writer and that *I'll write about this place.* I did say I would pay no more than the quoted $700. I would drive my van away (though my key hung from a hook on his wall behind the counter) and they could call the police if they wished. In fact, please do.

Two other customers watched me, perhaps entertained. Kyle wore a practiced poker face, not a tiny muscle of which had yet twitched. We stared at each other. I sensed victory. He said he'd "go through the numbers and see what he could do." After five minutes of crossing out and typing, and a new bill chugging out, he told me he'd been able to get it down to $750. I stomped out clutching my key, feeling utterly defeated in victory, having paid $750 for a tune-up. Well, I had new rear brakes and an emergency cable I might one day use. Maybe I'd honk at someone.

My van was surrounded by other cars, shining in the sun. The garage bays were empty. It struck me that all these parking-lot cars were decoys, brightly-painted mallards floating on this cement suburban pond, luring in foolish ducks like myself. Driving the two blocks home, I felt I was riding in a fragile creature, a victim of unwanted transplants.

That evening I phoned my parents, who had worried when I hadn't shown up. Again they murmured disapproval of my "letting all Ron's things go to waste," though there were still two days before the end of the month when his apartment had to be cleared out. It struck me how the elderly hate chaos, what they call "leaving things to the last minute." Maybe the notion of "the last minute" takes on fatal implications. I didn't explain my hesitations about weeding through

130

Ron's private stuff. Since his second wife left he'd been living alone for almost ten years. I didn't tell them that poking through my brother's things would feel like climbing right up into his angry armpit. I said I'd leave tomorrow morning and be there in the afternoon.

"Good," said my mother. "Ron really wants to see you."

In the morning when I started the van, stepped on the brake and put it in reverse to commence backing out, the brake pedal went *smish*, right to the floor. I *smished* it a few times in disbelief. I turned it off, got out, saw the thin stream of brake fluid running the length of the driveway to the reddish pool on the street.

This was good, this was comedy—$750 to have my brakes *broken*. What if I'd driven right out into traffic? I stomped inside, swearing and laughing. Leslie shook her head yelling, "You're kidding!" and little Lily started to cry. I phoned the garage. It wasn't Kyle, but in about twenty words I got my message across and the fellow, blandly apologetic, said a tow truck would be there soon. Lily was loud now and I could hardly hear myself demanding that the van be driven back to my house when it was fixed, and I wanted this done by lunch because I had a ferry to catch. I was all-business, macho, a new me. I'd never considered Ron a role model, and didn't now. Him looming up behind me, a smirking spectre, likely had to do with how much he'd occupied my thoughts lately. What would Ron have done? Well, he wouldn't have taken it *there* in the first place. And he wouldn't have given them a fucking *dime*. In fact, he would've just tuned 'er up himself.

Two that afternoon I called the garage asking where my car was. (I had to restrain Leslie from taking the phone and yelling at someone. She can do that sort of thing with ease.) The man checked and said it was just coming into the bay. I said I was promised noon, I said I needed to catch a ferry. I *almost* said something about needing to go see a dying brother.

The van was delivered at five. The driver, a kid, and oblivious to the history of injustice, was no-one to yell at. He seemed to expect thanks for this special service so I thanked him. He said, "Your right drum coupling wasn't on right, so out she came." He looked at me as if I should have known that.

I phoned my parents, tried to explain but ended up apologizing. Tomorrow, I promised. My mother got in that Ron had really wanted to see me today.

In the morning I repacked my day-bag and was throwing some rope into the van (I figured to bring back a chair or dresser of Ron's, if only for show) when Leslie hurried out with Lily in her arms. Lily had thrown up, had a high fever, and Leslie had arranged a quick visit with the doctor. She'd be back in an hour. I nodded and kissed Lily's hot little head. Leslie smiled sadly for me, knowing well my dealings with Ron and my parents, having heard about it so much. She looked big-eyed and feverish herself.

I went back inside to make myself breakfast. The phone rang as I was flipping eggs. It was my mother. Her voice sounded oddly full of strength.

"He's had another. We're at his hospital. They think this is it this time. It's affecting the swallowing and the breathing."

"Is it—I should—"

"You should be here right now."

I said I was on my way, and I hung up. Staring at the clock, my heart beating, I calculated doctors' waiting-rooms, traffic, ferries. Behind these calculations, something was weighing my desire: did I want see Ron die, or did I want to miss it?

But the comedy that had begun a few days ago was accelerating. Like *deus ex machina*, the phone rang again. It was Leslie and she was hysterical.

"*We almost—The car—almost killed us—These bastards—*"

"What's wrong? How's Lily? What happened?"

"*It was hardly running, and I was passing, right by so I turned in—It stalled—A truck had to screech to—We almost—*"

I got from her that they were at the red garage. I ran the five blocks. The van was parked haphazardly, at a diagonal, blocking two garage bays, the driver's door still open. I was huffing and dizzy as I pushed in the door. What I walked into instantly cleared my head.

My wife held Lily, who was red and mouth-breathing. Confronting the young man behind the counter, my wife was red too and breathing heavily herself. She had been yelling. The young man, a comedian wearing the overalls of someone named "Lisa," was smiling defensively.

"No, no. I worked on that van," he told her. "You're saying you want a tune-up?"

Spontaneously, my wife vomited. Angrily, her eyes on him. I don't know if her joining the comedy was deliberate. It's the kind of thing Leslie could probably do if she wished. But here in the aftermath stood "Lisa," and Leslie, and Lily, and me.

I think we'd all stopped breathing. In that second before anyone could move, the world was clarified.

Everyone has known a place that, for a moment, stands vastly, maybe religiously, crystal. Mine, my altar, was a garage waiting-room. I could feel the blood-pounding squeeze of shoes on my feet. Could register the three-headed candy machine with its glass offerings of cashews, sour fruits and jelly beans. I understood that my van's engine had been built in Asia. Could feel my complex hurry to see my dying brother, but would never know if he was worth hurrying to. Or if he had a sense of humour for bodies and cars breaking down, for the junk that lives do become. Here was feverish little Lily, my feelings for whom were untamed and sacred. Here was my wife, who likely had the flu herself but was possibly enjoying herself in ways I couldn't know. Here was this guy, "Lisa," who lacked training in what had just happened, and in what was happening now.

That is, clarity with no meaning to it at all. Lisa in control. This red garage.

The Maternity Suite

Caroline Adderson

THE RELUCTANT GRANDMOTHER

By dinner Betty was desperate, nerves bunched together like in that carnival game where you tug one of the hundred gathered strings to see what prize jumps. In this case, she was her own twitchy, jerky prize. Irritably, she tossed the shrimp in the cream sauce then spooned it over the pasta butterflies. The pepper mill, cranked, made the same sound as her teeth.

Carey tucked in the moment Betty set his plate down. Anna only winced. "Ma," she said. "I can't eat this."

"Why not?"

"Because. Because—"

Betty was about to leave right then, stalk off in a fury and light up—to hell with them!—except that Carey beat her to it. He lurched from the table and bolted out of the room. Down the hall the bathroom door slammed, but they could still hear his toilet-amplified retching. She turned to Anna. "What's the matter with Carey?"

"I'm going to have a baby!"

Instinctively, Betty pressed her hands to her own slack belly, a maternal salute. Eighteen months before, Pauline, her other daughter, had shown up unannounced after a year away in Mexico. When Betty opened the front door her uterus, completely docile since menopause, suddenly contracted. Yet it had taken her another full second to recognize Pauline on the step, tanned and eight months pregnant. Betty didn't like to think a reproductive organ might have an intelligence of its own.

"Anna," she said, tenderly, she hoped. "How far along are you?"

134

"About eight weeks." Anna put her face in her hands and began to sob.

"What? What's wrong?"

"Nothing. I'm happy. I can't stop crying, that's all. I cry all day long."

"That's normal." She meant hormones, though Anna had always been sentimental and easy to bring to tears. Taking Anna's plate to the counter, she scraped the pasta back into the pot, realizing then that the shrimp was what must have put Anna off. The clump of cells inside her would be about that colour, size and shape.

Carey reappeared, still looking queasy. "I told her," said Anna, holding out her hand to him. Startled, he glanced at Betty, turned crimson, then looked away. Guilty, Betty thought, and laughed out loud. *Nowadays they actually feel guilty for what they do to us.*

"He didn't know it would be like this," said Anna.

"Like what?"

"Sick-making," said Carey. "All my life if someone throws up, I throw up. I don't know how much more I can take."

"It's normal," Betty said again. She put a consoling arm around him, her favourite son-in-law—her only one.

Two years before, Betty's husband Robert had rejoined the flock. Thursday afternoons the little Reverend would arrive looking every inch his denomination in corduroys and zeal. He met Robert in his room, the one that used to be the den when Robert could climb stairs, actually got him out of bed and cross-legged on the floor seemingly by murmuring appeasements to his pain. The Light of Christ was a radiant presence in the room, Betty had learned listening outside the door. "Inhale. With every breath you are filled with Healing Light." She brought in tea and Robert's medication on a tray, marvelling because the little Reverend was so gay. Robert had used to refer to the United Church as "The Church of the Perverts."

At least the Reverend could take credit for making a better smoker out of Betty. Standing on the patio after Anna and Carey had gone home, she inhaled with fervour, paused ecstatically, then blew a pillar of smoke above her head, all the way to heaven. A mid-July evening, warm, the garden climaxing in tufts and pouches, cups, bells, horns, spires, bristles, balls, stars. She unwound and turned on the hose, aiming the sprinkling nozzle low at the impatiens in the shaded bed along the fence. Her children forbade her to smoke. Cancer had mouldered away their father and now they began their visits with an inspection of her home, sniffing room-to-room, checking potted plants for butts, not letting her out of sight. Today Anna had found a disposable lighter in the liquor cabinet and, with a shriek, had thrown it on the living-room carpet. The very sight of the gaudy blue cylinder set off a Pavlovian response in Betty, her cravings worsening through the afternoon until nicotine stained everything, even Anna's happy news. So crabbed by the time Anna blurted her announcement, Betty's first thought had been a sour wondering what Carey and Anna would raise a child on. Anna had never finished her degree. Carey languished on some substitute list and when he taught, it was only English to refugees. How lucrative could that be?

Water pooled around the impatiens drooping from the day's heat. Soon they would perk as Betty, her cigarette half-smoked, was perking now. She tugged on the hose, raised and swung the nozzle around to the sunny wall of the house. The water, soaring above her in a parabola, caught the light and for a dazzling, prismatic moment became a sheen of rainbow against the white stucco wall. Mist hit her, pinging cold against her face and arms. Then a feeling, too, showered down, a tingling.

Joy for her daughter, at last.

The phone rang after midnight. When Betty answered, it was to a hiss. "You're smoking, aren't you?" Then Pauline's real voice asked, "Did Anna tell you?"

"Yes."

"She just wants a baby because I have Rebecca. She always has to have what I have."

"That's unkind," Betty chided, though the very thought had crossed her own mind earlier, before she'd had that cigarette. She could hear the supposedly coveted Rebecca in the background, Rebecca or a siren, and wondered if Pauline ever put the child to bed or just let her cry herself to sleep behind the television.

Pauline was really calling, she said, to tell Betty about the dream she'd had the night before. "Me and Anna went to visit you in the hospital because you'd had a baby. Except when we got there, we found out you'd actually had a cat. The weird thing was the cat didn't surprise us at all. We just wondered why it was full-grown and not a kitten. Different gestation periods I guess. Nine months is probably way more time than you need for a kitten. Do you think I dreamed it because of Smitty?"

Smitty was Pauline's grey and black six-toed tabby, a biter. Since Rebecca had started walking, Smitty had begun stalking. Naturally, Betty had advised neutering. The world, in Betty's opinion, would be a better place if everyone were neutered. "Have you taken him to the vet yet?" she asked.

"How's this for a coincidence? The same day Anna announces she's knocked up, Smitty gets his balls chopped off!"

Laughing, Betty said goodnight. After she hung up, she stared for a moment at the still-life arrangement on the bedside table: *Nature morte avec telephone et fruits.* Anna had put the fruit bowl there so Betty could nibble away her late night cravings. Fruit of my womb, she thought, holding up a waxy red apple. In her other hand, she held an orange.

Pauline was born tangled in umbilical cord and with her first shrill and indignant vocalization seemed to announce that she would never be tied up or down again. Then, as if anyone could have mistaken her meaning, she continued screaming for three months. It was a demand for love fiercer than Betty had ever imagined. Her nipples cracked from giving and Pauline drew her blood.

Anna was the quiet one, so placid she was cast as the Infant Jesus in the United Church nativity play where previously they had used a big bald doll. Pauline, three years old that Christmas, flossy in her lamb's suit, clustered with the rest of the pre-school flock around Anna in the manger. Betty and Robert could hear her crying, "Meow," while everyone else bleated. At home after the service, Pauline insisted Anna be put to bed in a box in the garage.

In later years, Anna graduated to playing Mary. Pauline had no further interest in Sunday school theatrics; the days and nights of her real life provided drama enough. Her pre-teen vocational aspiration was to be a bank robber, so she shoplifted for practice and got caught. Robert, in charge of discipline, of disciplining Pauline, grounded her for a year. This didn't stop the boys from coming. So skinny, shaggy and sullen, all wearing the same grey hooded sweatshirts as they filed down to the rumpus-room, they reminded Betty of a chain gang. She strongly suspected Pauline had relinquished her virginity at thirteen, probably in their own basement, though she could never bring herself to ask. Who could she blame for her daughter's loss? She and Robert were decent people. They had faults, certainly; they played too much bridge, for example, but they had never modelled lust.

She remembered Pauline showing her an advertisement in *Teen*. "What's Tampax?" She was only ten at the time, too young, Betty thought, to know how tedious her fate would be. "I wish," Betty had answered, "you wouldn't read those magazines."

So perhaps her own prudishness had contributed to Pauline's preternatural curiosity. She vowed to do better by Anna. "Inside a woman's body is a nest," she told her and from Anna's perplexed look Betty knew she was thinking of twigs and grass and tangled bits of string.

"It's made of blood."

Anna's bottom lip began to quiver. "I know! Pauline told me, but I hoped it wasn't true!"

Anna being prettier than Pauline, taller and fair, Betty had expected from her an even longer line of convict suitors. They never came. On Friday nights Anna went to the library with her girlfriends. She joined a swim club and spent every weekend at the pool or painting watercolour pictures of butterflies and flowers in her room. Into adolescence she sailed on gentle breezes. When she was fourteen, she woke up screaming.

Robert drove. Betty sat in the back seat with Anna's head, damp with sweat, cradled in her lap, Anna moaning, panting and clutching her abdomen.

In a curtained off corner of the emergency-room, Betty helped a nurse strip Anna and get her into the flimsy gown. She hadn't meant to look at her daughter's naked body, but glimpsed, in spite of herself, pubic hair and a white tympanum of belly, round and taut. The doctor, when he at last appeared, kneaded Anna pitilessly where her pain was. "How old are you?" he asked and when Anna answered through gritted teeth, he glanced at Betty. "Could she be pregnant, do you think?"

Anna wailed.

"Now, now," he said perfunctorily. "These things happen. Let me have a look."

It was what Betty had always feared, of course, but from Pauline. Her ashamed face in her hands, she heard their bustling preparations: the snap of a rubber glove, a scraping chair, then the odd "Oh!" from the doctor. She looked up to see Anna's feet in the stirrups. The doctor had vanished. The nurse, smiling down on Betty, said, "Don't worry. She'll be fine," and hurried out leaving Betty alone with Anna. If only Robert were here, Betty thought, though she was also relieved that he was not. It was a female crisis. His proper place was behind the steering-wheel and, now, in the waiting-room— Robert instinctively understood this. Still, she could have used him to raise Cain with the staff.

Leaning over Anna, Betty asked her coldly, "Who did this to you?" but Anna only whimpered and shook her head. Betty recalled then an article in one of Pauline's magazines. It usually happened to girls skinny like Anna, or girls disguised by fat—either way, it didn't show—girls, good and confused, who had no idea what sex was. Had some boy asked her to close her eyes, insisting it was his finger? Or worse, some grown-up lech. A teacher?

"You should tell me things!"

"What things?" Anna sobbed.

Suddenly the narrow space at the end of the bed accommodated a crowd—the nurse and doctor, interns, and Dr. So-and-so, barely introduced, from Ob-Gyn. They opened Anna's legs like a textbook and immediately began to thrill. The gynae-

139

cologist said something about a "membrane" and someone else pointed out the "bulge." These words together offended Betty, as did the faces gaping, via the speculum, in her daughter's deepest, most private place. Behind the curtains like this, she was reminded of a freak-show tent or a travelling brothel in the desert. She jerked the sheet down over Anna's spread legs.

"What is going on?"

It was the farthest thing from a baby. Rare, but not serious: an imperforated hymen. Menstrual blood had been accumulating inside Anna for months.

Betty walked beside the stretcher as it coursed the antiseptic halls. No-one could be purer than Anna, she was thinking. They could operate, puncture her with their instruments, but never penetrate her innocence. This was the kind of romantic nonsense she could entertain during a crisis. Afterward, she wouldn't even remember thinking it.

At the end of her third month Anna asked Betty to come and help her paint the room that would be the nursery. No more than a glorified closet, up to now it had been their study. Betty took the pictures off the walls. They folded up the trestle desk, moved it and the blue plastic Ikea chair into the bedroom, then set to clearing the bookshelves of the pregnancy guides and all the texts that were the evidence of Anna's flighty university career: psychology, anthropology, art history. Lugging an armload into the bedroom, Betty paused to read the title on the first huge volume and wondered how anyone could be so wordy on the irrelevant subject of Flemish painting.

In the tiny kitchen, she made tea. Anna staggered through, a tower of books in her arms, strands of blond hair escaping from her ponytail—glowing, Betty had to admit. She looked like the Madonna on the cover of the textbook. "You'd better be careful," she warned. "Let's take a break."

"How did you feel when you were pregnant with me, Ma?"

Betty passed her a mug of tea. "I don't remember."

"How can you not remember?"

"We didn't make a fuss like you."

"Who's making a fuss?"

"You and Pauline. Back then you'd be as big as a house and no-one would pass comment."

"Daddy wasn't with you, I guess."

"In the delivery-room?" Betty snorted. "Certainly not. The only good thing about men in delivery-rooms is a declining birth rate."

"Oh, Ma!"

Overpopulation had been one of Betty and Robert's "topics." On this very subject they'd spent many a pleasurable evening agreeing with each other in outraged tones. Betty told Anna, "Only in developed countries is the birth rate dropping. Only in developed countries are men looking where they shouldn't. Why would you want Carey to see you like that?"

"It's beautiful."

"Ach!" Betty set down her mug, exasperated. All Pauline and Anna talked about now, lounging in Betty's backyard and sipping endless blender drinks, was the glory of nausea and stretch marks. Rebecca, meanwhile, the product of Pauline's nine months of masochistic indulgence, toddled unheeded through the flowerbeds eating dirt. What Betty was thankful for at least: they finally had something in common. It used to be that whenever they got near one another, Pauline would drop a rose and run. If Anna so much as looked the wrong way at Pauline, Pauline would fly at her shrieking "Noogie!" and grate her knuckles mercilessly across Anna's skull. This, even after they had both finished high school and ought to have been comporting themselves like adults. Now, finally, after all these years, they were acting sisterly.

Anna asked, accusing, "Did you smoke?"

"Yes, I smoked. Nobody told us not to."

"I might have been damaged, you know."

"Well, you weren't." Betty drained her mug and stood. "Okay. Let's paint."

In the little room, Anna knelt to pry open one of the cans with a screwdriver.

"Is Carey working today?" Betty asked.

"I don't know."

"Why isn't he helping?"

"He's not very useful," said Anna with a sigh.

Why marry then, thought Betty, if not to have a live-in painter, plumber and small appliance repairman? But she didn't say it; a blade had appeared on her tongue the second Anna mentioned smoking. She did love Carey, just not as much as cigarettes.

The lid popped off the can. "Is that the colour you want?" asked Betty, dubious.

Anna stirred the paint, then tipped the can and let it pour, a rich, warm stream into the rolling tray. "I think it's going to be a girl."

Betty said, "I'd call that red."

That night she went through the photo albums, but could only find one picture of herself pregnant. Black and white, it showed her and Pauline hand-in-hand against a backdrop of shadowy trees, her body half-turned away from Pauline, her face to the camera. Visible in profile under her cotton sundress was the bulge of Anna. Where had she got that dress? She couldn't remember being so feminine. Burly, energetic, she had spent most of her youth in trousers, like a girl in one of those old Workers' Party posters with a pole over her shoulder and a huge red flag unfurling behind.

With Pauline she squabbled endlessly over feminism. According to Pauline, every problem a woman faced was the fault of men. Her own hypocritical consorting with the oppressor she rationalized away with semantics. Pauline did not say "men." She said "the patriarchy." Naturally, no-one epitomized the patriarchy for Pauline more than poor Robert, who was only fulfilling his responsibilities. Betty felt sorry for men today, she really did. How confused they must be!

"Bladder infections," Pauline gave as an example. Busy tending selflessly to the needs of others, women neglected to take the time to void.

"What rubbish!" Betty had crowed. "Have you ever heard of self-control?"

Evidently not, for Pauline couldn't even name the culprit who had knocked her up in Mexico. Betty, though, was of that stalwart generation that could hold its urine all day if it had to. If hunger needled her, she looked at her watch, decided when to eat, and felt not a pang until that time. Even when Robert had crept across the ravine of decency that separated their twin beds, she never let go of the reins of her senses. She focused instead on the ingredients and steps for making bouillabaisse.

But at times in her life the flag behind her had changed from red to white—an unconditional surrender—in pregnancy and, later, when menopause vanquished her, just as cancer had Robert. With the little Reverend at his side, Robert had battled against his dying body, but his body had won. Now that he was gone, Betty carried on the struggle, faced the same surly foe, clad now not in the armour of disease, but of craving. She couldn't even lay out a game of solitaire without a fight.

She closed the photo album, returned it to the shelf, left the den and climbed the stairs. Undressing for bed, she paused before the dresser mirror with her nightgown in her hand. The enemy's other guise was age. Her breasts had flattened, skin sagged all over like a too-large garment.

"We are a will," she said out loud, "dressed up in a body."

The telephone rang. Naked, Betty crossed over to the bedside table to the two remaining apples in the bowl. On the third ring, she slid her fingers under the phone and drew out the cigarette. The phone shrilled, a proxy. Ignoring it, she wandered the room, cigarette defiantly between her lips. She was searching, searching for the lighter she had hid.

THE EXPECTANT MOTHER

The professor was explaining something marvellous a little monk had done with sweet peas. Closing her eyes, Anna pictured the sweet peas that every summer scaled the fence in their yard, a tangle of moth-winged blooms, some pink, others red or mauve or white. As a girl she believed Jesus made dawn rounds through the garden with a brush and palette, mixing paints with dew. Now, at twenty, that was the explanation she still preferred. Science was not saving her father. All it had done was disillusion her.

Someone poked her with a pencil. Starting, she turned to face the smirk of the person sitting next to her. He had a long neck prominently knobbed with an Adam's apple and straight hair parted down the middle, neither blonde nor brown, but some sheenless shade between. "When it comes to genes," he said, "Levi Strauss is still the man for me."

"My father has cancer." She began to cry and Carey to panic —something that would happen again and again until they were married, and after, too.

"Do you want to talk?" he asked her. "Do you want to get out of here? Hey, let's get out of here." He stuffed his notebook into his army satchel and took her by the hand. Tripping and premature, their exit. The professor at the front of the hall droned on. Probably he was thinking his words were having no effect, but he was wrong, for instead of a veil she'd worn a wreath of sweet peas on her head. They were married in her parent's back yard just weeks before her father died. Reverend Chalmer conducted the ceremony, her father's wish, not Anna's. Also present were Carey's mother from Nova Scotia, who turned out to be as awful as Carey had claimed, and a few of Anna's high school friends. Pauline was in Mexico living loosely under the sun.

The reception afterward was at The Teahouse. "If only that woman weren't so morose," Betty had told Anna in the washroom as they reapplied their lipstick. She meant Carey's mother. "You'd think she was paying."

"If only Pauline had come," said Anna, solely to remind her mother of the slight.

"That, too."

"If only Daddy would get better!"

"Stop it," said Betty sharply.

Her father hadn't been able to give her away properly, but had waited in a wheelchair by the birdbath while Anna had walked the green aisle of the lawn alone. When he took her hand and squeezed, it was with the last of his strength.

"I wish we'd had a different minister."

"Enough!" Betty shooed Anna out of the washroom, staying behind a few minutes herself—to smoke. Anna wasn't fooled.

During prenuptial counselling Reverend Chalmer had seemed to suggest they shouldn't marry. First, he'd insinuated that student loans would undo them. Couldn't they wait until they had finished school and were more financially stable?

"No," was Anna's flat reply.

He talked about maturity. They were only in their early twenties. Did they really know if they were.... He searched a long time for the right word. Compatible? Anna reddened. What was the Reverend getting at? He wasn't married. What did he know? But in the end, he agreed to unite them, did it with pleasure, seemingly, as if his reservations were the petals that had been tossed as confetti. At dinner he even raised his glass to toast them. "If you ever have a need, come and see me," Anna overheard him tell Carey.

"God give you love," was his toast.

As soon as Robert died, Anna dropped out of university. A bride of less than a month, it should have been the happiest time of her life. Instead she couldn't stop crying. She became like one of those mourners for hire, grieving for all concerned: for the stoical Betty, for Carey, who didn't know Robert well enough to care, and for Pauline who wasn't even there. Carey was very patient with her during these months. When she woke crying in the night he would hold her and stroke her hair. He understood her reluctance to begin marital relations, preoccupied as she was with Robert's illness and then his passing. He said it was a relief to him.

Countless times during childhood Anna had envisioned a funeral, but it was always Pauline's. In her imagination, she threw herself on the open casket, on top of Pauline, as cold in death as she had been in life, hearing between her sobs the other mourners praising her and castigating Pauline for her heartlessness. It wasn't so much her sister's death that she wished for, as recognition for what she had suffered as her father's favourite. And, of course, relief from Pauline's bully presence, which Mexico had at least provided.

When she heard Pauline was back though, Anna rushed right over with Carey. She wanted to show Pauline Carey. Confronted with her sister's condition, Anna was scandalized and Pauline, sensing it, only flaunted her Queen-sized self all the more. With her feet up on the coffee table, she commanded them with a fluttering hand: a cup of tea, a hot water bottle, her slippers off. When they were not scurrying back and forth to run her errands, two of them were required to heave her off the couch so she could go to the bathroom. Pauline had pulled a fast one on them all, Anna realized. Automatically she had earned the solicitude of everyone, despite how selfishly she had behaved. It wasn't fair. Pauline hadn't even apologized for not coming back for the wedding. She hadn't mentioned Robert once.

Then the unexpected happened. After almost two days of labour, Pauline produced 9 lbs. 7 oz. of healthy baby girl. The family reunited around her hospital bed waiting for the nurse to fetch Rebecca, listening to the details of Pauline's ordeal as she wolfed food off the meal tray. She claimed to be stitched from stem to stern. The white of one of her eyes had filled with blood. Pausing only to tear the foil top off the pudding cup, Pauline happened to glance up. Anna was looking at Pauline so did not at first realize that the door to the room, which was behind her, had opened and the nurse was wheeling in the bassinet. What she saw was the besotted smile suddenly bloom on Pauline's face.

She would not let any of them hold Rebecca. Clutching her tight, cooing feverishly, she consented only to opening the blanket that swaddled her so that they might get a better peek. "Isn't she a little dear!" cried Betty. Anna almost burst into tears. She thought she'd never seen anything as beautiful as that rosy face with its pursed, petal lips squeezed between the rounds of her cheeks.

The next day, when Pauline came home, Anna and Carey went over to help out, as they did almost every day for the next six weeks. Betty was the only one with any experience but, as Carey pointed out, it was almost a quarter-century out of date. He took on the job of reading aloud from the manual. Pauline slept between feedings. Betty and Anna, holding the baby in turns, could not believe the change in Pauline. If she had turned to stone they would have been less surprised because stone would have been in character.

Of course, it was not just Pauline who had changed. The whole family had been brought together as they never had been before, not even when Robert was dying. Anna, who had always believed in miracles anyway, took this very much to heart.

In the three blocks that she'd walked from the naturopath, every passer-by met her eye and smiled. Her hands in her pockets, she could feel through the lining of her coat the not-so-secret swell. The baby was fully formed inside her now, but only six inches long, its skin transparent, in her imagination radiant, like the little dove in the Van Eyck Annunciation.

She crossed the street to the deli. The naturopath had recommended she start massaging her perineum with olive oil, but as she stepped inside, goat bells clanking her entrance, the aroma made her instantly ravenous and she went straight over to the pastry case instead. Pressing her belly into the glass, she gazed down at the trays of diamond-cut baklava, the little bales of shredded wheat sopped with honey, until a man with a large nose and very black Einstein hair came over. "Bea-u-ti-ful la-dy." He moved his hands in the air, juggling the syllables. "How can I help you?"

Anna pointed through the glass. "Two pieces."

"Two?" He winked. "For me and for you?"

"For me and my husband."

"Husband?" The knife snatched up, he aimed it at his heart, abruptly detouring into the pastry case and, with the tip, sliding the baklava into a paper envelope. Anna hesitated. "Maybe another for the bus."

Approving, he tucked a third piece in. "An even number is better. Why not four?"

"All right." She was just so hungry all the time. Taking the envelope from him, she asked, "Where's your olive oil?"

"Ah! I will take you to the olive grove myself." He came out from behind the counter and swaggered on ahead, apron strings tied in a droopy bow over the empty seat of his pants. Down an aisle of coffee and grape leaves she followed, past red-eyed olives suspended in vinegar and black olives in an open vat. The oil was displayed across three shelves—yellow, gold, amber, green.

"This is best. This is for you." He reached for a small bottle, the deepest of the greens, and placed it in her hands. "This is extra virgin."

"What happened to me," Pauline told Anna, "was every time I sneezed, I peed. A line appeared from here to here. The *linea negra*, right? Also, I felt happy. I realized I'd never been happy in all my life."

It did not occur to Anna to ask the reason for her sister's chronic unhappiness. All she wondered was why she didn't have a line down her own belly like Pauline had had. Before she could ask what exactly it had looked like, Pauline sat up from where she'd been stretched out on the couch licking honey off her fingers. "Where's Rebecca? Rebecca!"

The little girl came teetering around the corner, all pink gums and wide-spaced teeth. Anna didn't like her toddler smile or cobweb hair, or the ugly red scratches on her arms and face. She had been such a perfect baby; it was a pity. Looking elsewhere instead, to the kitchen, Anna saw the cat. Striped, broad in the paw, it was the reason Pauline had come over unannounced and eaten the last piece of baklava, the one Anna was saving for Carey: she was here to dump it on them. Pupils dilated, fixed blackly on the child, it was inching forward, low against the carpet.

Uh oh, Anna thought.

It joggled side-to-side then darted, reared up and boxed Rebecca twice. Rebecca stood there stunned. "Smitty!" Pauline screamed, setting off the child. "Fuck you, Smitty!" She turned accusingly to Anna. "You see why you've got to take him?"

"But what about when our baby comes?"

"By then Rebecca will be old enough to bash him back. Hush, baby. Hush." She scooped up the sobbing child and began to bounce her—roughly Anna thought.

Anna went to the bedroom, returning a moment later with a book. Pauline was trying to wipe Rebecca's face with her sweatshirt sleeve, streaking a slug-trail of mucous along it, Rebecca still wailing. "Enough!" Pauline thunked her down.

Rebecca followed Pauline back to the couch, frantic arms stretched out. "What do you want? You want a tittie?" Swinging her onto her knee, she runched up her sweatshirt; a breast came tumbling out.

"It says here somewhere," said Anna, scanning the index of the book, "that I should stay away from cats. I could catch something."

"That's only if you mess around with the litter box. Carey can change the litter box. Where is Carey?"

"He'll be home soon. He got a three month contract, did I tell you?" She was searching the columns for *linea negra*.

"Do your breasts hurt?" asked Pauline.

Anna looked up. "Did yours?"

"They throbbed."

"They hurt a little," she said, patting at herself. "What about that line?"

"It looked like eye-liner. I thought it was where they would cut me open, if it came to that."

By the time they heard Carey come in, Rebecca had fallen asleep nursing, her wispy head thrown back on Pauline's thigh, air percolating through blocked nostrils.

"Ah!" he said from the doorway when he saw the child. Coming straight over, he sat on the edge of the coffee table and leaned over her, stage whispering, "Becky. Little Beck-Beck. Who's your papa? Who's your daddy? It's all right. You can tell me."

Pauline laughed. Carey was allowed to joke like this but when Anna or their mother asked, Pauline flipped. She had probably slept with a lot of Mexicans—Anna shuddered at the thought—except Rebecca was so colourless, it seemed an unlikely paternity. The little girl looked as if she were kept in a closet half the time.

Carey pressed Rebecca's nose, blinked a moment at his finger before wiping it on his sweater front, then went into the bedroom to change his clothes. He liked children, Anna knew he did. Even her mother had said he would make a good father. "He's wonderful with Pauline's bastard," were her words.

"Are you staying for supper?" Anna asked Pauline.

In the bedroom, Carey screamed a second before Smitty came tearing out. Pauline got hurriedly to her feet, Rebecca flopping in her arms. "No," she said. "We better go."

Carey, after Pauline had left, said he didn't know what hit him or, more precisely, what had seized his Achilles' tendon and sunk in its teeth. It was a surprising reaction because usually when Carey was angry he just hunkered down and refused to speak.

"First you spring a baby on me and now this kamikaze cat!"

"Why?" Anna cried in renewed torment. "Why don't you want the baby?"

Carey punched the wall, hard enough that he winced.

"People are starting to wonder!" she told him.

"Wonder *what*?"

"Why you aren't helping!"

"What people?" he screamed.

"Ma! She thought it was strange you weren't there to paint the nursery!"

Sneeringly, Carey laughed. "That's not a nursery. That's a room in a bordello."

It was where she ran to, where she always went now when they had a fight. Her back against the wall, she slid down it, then collapsed onto her side, sobbing, but with gulping pauses in between so she could hear Carey's approaching steps. After a few minutes, she rolled over onto her back, her sobs directed outward instead of muffled by the carpet. Soon she began to whimper instead of cry, but gave that up, too, eventually, and just lay there on the floor of the empty room watching the walls pulse all around her.

The door pushed open finally and Smitty came padding in. Thrumming in his throat, he rubbed the whole smooth length of himself across her face still wet with tears.

"Carey?" she called, picking fur out of her mouth. "Carey?"

At least he still went with her to their childbirth classes. He enjoyed them because, out of all the husbands, he was the only comedian. During the first class, Judy, the instructor, had passed around a pink plush fetus held by Velcro inside a cloth uterus.

"This is a good model because, like us, it's three dimensional and soft."

"And in winter," Carey added, "it doubles as a toque!" He tore out the fetus and popped the uterus on his head, cracking up the class.

When a worried woman asked, "What if we lose our baby?" Carey had piped up with the suggestion that she pin her phone number to its diaper. Everyone laughed again. They didn't know how things were at home. They thought he was funny all the time.

Tonight Anna lay on the blue vinyl exercise mat to do the breathing exercises. A nervous fluttering began inside her, like small wings beating back and forth. She grabbed Carey's hand. The room was full of people. He couldn't very well pull away this time.

"There." She pressed his hand to her belly. "Do you feel it?"

From the relaxation tape: the sound of surf and plainting gulls, the low murmur of rain, then a fog horn's hollow echo. Were there any sadder sounds in the world? The men were all kneeling beside their wives, rubbing the women's temples in the slow and gentle circles Judy had taught. But Carey just stared down at Anna, on his face an indeterminate expression, more than one feeling, none very nice.

When they had put away the mats, Judy said, "Let's talk about sex. After all, that's how you got into this mess in the first place."

Everyone turned to Carey, waiting for the wisecrack.

Undressing for her bath, Anna stepped gingerly out of her panties, looked down and knew at once she would have to start to pray again. She should have started sooner. She hoped it was not too late.

This was something nobody knew about, not even her mother or Carey, certainly not Pauline. As a girl she used to build altars, then collect butts from the ashtrays, amassing the stale tobacco threads to burn on them. Sometimes her ceremonies included a live beetle crucified on a pin and slaps she would give herself. Also, she had to refrain from unclean thoughts and picture everything perfect and neat. Before bed each night she would open the Bible at random and memorize the line under her finger no matter what little sense it made, which was where she had got the notion of thoughts being clean or unclean in the first place. If she did all these things, then her prayers would be answered. She won two swim meets this way and did not get warts, despite Pauline holding her down and noogying her infected knuckles all over Anna's face. It was through prayer, too, that she had been able to delay getting her first period by two years. All the other girls had started by age twelve, but Anna had been fourteen.

She stoppered the drain, turned on the cold water and watched the basin fill. Would it have smoothed things, she wondered, if she had told all this to Reverend Chalmer? Maybe he would have liked her more if he had known how pious she could be. Looking back, she felt as if he had put a curse on them.

She picked the panties off the floor, bending almost an effort now, and tossed them in the basin. For a minute they floated on the surface of the water until, saturated, their own weight made them sink. White in the white porcelain, soon they settled under the water where the stain loosened and began to lift. Slowly, it floated upward, a single plume, like red smoke drifting.

The Suspecting Father

Carey's worst memory was of his mother with a Q-tip. In dreams his profound dread of it would magnify to her coming at him with a majorette's baton, cotton-tipped. For years and years he had stood it. He had thought it was a ritual that went on in the home of every boy, that after your Sunday night bath your mother would come in and sit on the edge of the tub and, cringing with disgust, clean under your foreskin while you stood shivering on the bathmat. Then he started junior high school, all the naked boys crammed into one big shower stall. He was the only one born in Scotland. Unless you were born in Scotland, he discovered, you didn't even have a foreskin.

He began to lock the door. "Carey?" she would call. "What are you doing in there, Carey?" She probably thought he was abusing himself. She had told him many times, "Carey, never abuse yourself," and he was thrown into confusion. What would she call forcing a cotton-swab into the hood of his penis? Hygiene, of course. She had been a nurse until Carey's father had brought her to Canada. Eventually she let him be, but ever after on a Sunday night she would leave the Q-tip in a saucer on the vanity.

When the time came for him to go to university, he chose a school as far away as possible from his mother, went from one coast to the other. Every Sunday night she phoned and asked if he was meeting girls, which he was. He wasn't particularly handsome, but what attracted women more than looks he quickly learned, was a sense of humour, preferably self-deprecating, and a certain wistfulness. He would date them until that first sweet kiss, then abandon them and not return their perplexed calls. His mother never asked if he were keeping himself clean, but that was implied by the very time and day she phoned.

How, then, had he found himself married? Very quickly, it seemed now. Beside him in one of his classes had sat the same extraordinarily beautiful young woman day in and out. She did not seem to notice him and, at first, he thought this was because she was used to being stared at, used to her attention being subtly and not so subtly sought. As the weeks went on though, he decided she was simply preoccupied. When he finally spoke to her—what a windfall! She actually took him home.

It was to what he saw that afternoon that he let himself be married: an old house filled with plants and brimming ash-trays, half-finished games of Solitaire, books, the coffee-table stained in interlocking rings from years of G&Ts, CBC chattering in the background, crossword puzzles, dust. Outside in her garden Betty, Anna's mother, greeted them with a finger to her lips alongside a dangling cigarette. "Your father's asleep." He was taken into the den to see Robert on a hospital bed, wincing so nobly in his drugged dreams that Carey pictured his own father dying that way, though in reality, he'd been killed in a mine accident, instantly, when Carey was an infant. Later a minister visited, just like a vicar in an English novel, and closed himself up with Robert. There was also a sister, he learned, but she was wayward. Wayward. How perfect!

He began to spend part of every day there. No coffee spoons with the family crest were polished for him. Instead, he was handed a book on composting and the latest issue of *Maclean's* and told to read to Robert until he fell back asleep. Over dinner, Betty expounded her mad-cap take on world events, French cooking, and how she would just love to try Robert's morphine if only she were sure not to end up like the junkie mother in that O'Neill play. Completely sexless was Betty, always in pants, thick waisted with a muscular-looking hump of fat across her back—an ideal woman, Carey thought. He hoped Anna would turn out like that.

Anna was the one who proposed that they marry. She said, "It would mean so much to Daddy and we don't know how much time he has left." Maybe Carey thought he loved her. He certainly felt a surge of something for her when he introduced her to his mother and saw how absolutely she disapproved. At that point, two days before the wedding, he might have changed his mind, but he so badly wanted to defy and disappoint. Of course, in agreeing to marry Anna, it had also occurred to him that wherever he went with Anna he would be envied by other men, men who were once boys capering in the shower, pointing and laughing at his foreskin.

How quickly everything changed. The old man died, Betty withdrew and Anna's sister reappeared, hugely pregnant. Anna's sister, he had been led to understand, was quite a piece of work. What the hell was Anna then? Carey was soon to wonder.

Though Anna spent most of her time at her mother's, he tried to be home as little as possible. Happily inexperienced as a teacher, it took him hours to prepare his lessons. Afterward, he would go for coffee and read the paper at leisure and sometimes take in a movie, too.

As he was settling at a window table with the classified section, someone said hello. Looking up, Carey saw a man neatly dressed in a jacket and cords. At first he didn't recognize, not without the collar, the man ultimately responsible for fucking up his life.

"And a hearty congratulations. I heard your news."

The Reverend switched hands that held his paper cup, extending the right. When Carey took it, it felt small and exceedingly warm, or maybe it was just that Carey was blushing so hotly.

"May I join you?"

Carey hastened to make room on the tiny tabletop even as he screamed *No, no, no* in his head. The Reverend set down his cup and, taking off his jacket, folded it neatly over the back of the chair. He fingered his shirt cuffs unhurriedly before sitting down and carefully removing the plastic lid on his coffee. All the while Carey felt the same fidgety dread, as he had back in pre-nuptial counselling when it had seemed to take the Reverend forever to formulate what he was going to say—mingled now with fury. Then Carey remembered *what* the Reverend had said; the sense of relief was overwhelming. The Reverend, bless his heart, had tried to warn him.

"Betty says you're all very excited. It's March, right?"

"What?"

"When the baby comes. Your life is about to change forever. What a wonderful thing." Chuckling, he told Carey, "Remember, we still do christenings."

"Can I ask your advice about something, Reverend?"

"Please," he said. "And please call me Brian."

"Brian. It's about a friend of mine. He's in a—Well, it's a similar situation, but it's not me. I mean—" Carey snapped his biscotti in half. "I met him at the childbirth class we're taking. His wife is pregnant, too."

Reverend Chalmer, Brian, leaned back in the chair, listening.

"The thing is, his wife is going to have a baby, but the baby isn't his."

The Reverend's delicate brows jerked up momentarily.

"The baby isn't his," Carey said again.

"You mean his wife had relations with another man and became pregnant?"

"Yes."

"How does he know this?"

"What?" asked Carey.

"How does he know the baby isn't his? Even if his wife had relations with another man, the baby could still be your friend's."

"It isn't. They weren't—" Eyes averted, he took a sip of coffee. "They weren't having relations. That's what he told me."

"Oh," said the Reverend, sounding pained. He looked out the window.

"What should he do?"

"There's a child involved. I advise forgiveness."

Carey bristled. "But she did this and now she acts like nothing is the matter! She won't even admit to it!"

The Reverend stalled between a shake of his head and a nod. "It's a difficult situation, I agree, but I still recommend forgiveness for the sake of the child. And counselling, of course."

"Don't you do annulments anymore?" Carey asked sarcastically.

The Reverend opened his hands in apology. "There's divorce."

One night Carey screamed so long and loud at Anna that a blood vessel exploded in his nose. A gory bib down his sweater front, he pinched his nostrils and, head thrown back, let Anna lead him to the bathroom. While he sat on the tub's edge, she washed the sticky blood off his face and neck. "Why?" he begged her, grabbing the hand that held the cloth. "Why did you do this to me?"

"I didn't do anything. You were the one yelling."

"That's not what I mean. I'll never forgive you, you know."

"It's just a nosebleed," Anna tsked.

He wondered then, he seriously wondered, if she was even right in the head.

When he ran into the Reverend earlier that week, he had been about to search the classifieds for an apartment. What had stopped him from doing so before was shame. He was so ashamed. If he left Anna, people would ask her why. Betty would certainly ask, and Pauline. One question would lead to another and before long everyone would know that their marriage had remained unconsummated. He would be blamed, of course. The man always was. As Anna's condition grew more obvious, the situation became intolerable; the taunt, in effect, was worse now than his shame. He couldn't live with Anna another minute. After the Reverend left Starbucks though, Carey did not pick up the paper again. He drank his coffee slowly, reflecting on what the Reverend had said.

The next day he told his students, half in pantomime, that his wife was pregnant. He thought it might help him if he admitted to it, but their jubilant congratulations only embarrassed him and he immediately wished he'd hadn't. Worse, a few days later he came in and found a large, flatish, rectangular box covering the whole desktop. Crowding around, they insisted that he open it. "For your will be born baby," read the card.

"Oh, fuck," Carey groaned and they understood because swear words are the first words everybody learns.

He tore off the paper. Inside was a crib. He could barely stammer thank you. So moved was he by their generosity that he took on their inarticulacy. Most of them had arrived here penniless from the desperate places they had fled; there was a Bosnian couple, several Kurds from Iraq, a six-foot Sudanese, three Afghan women in headscarves, a Burmese and a stunned little Sri Lankan girl with a bindi and only one pronoun. Their own children had fallen asleep to the lullaby of war, but for their teacher's child they wished something safe, new and white with a vinyl-covered mattress and bars the regulation distance apart. Humbled as well as touched, Carey tried to think of something he might have done and felt proud of, but he could not see past how he had been torturing Anna. He had always thought of himself as a nice guy. Everyone did. Maybe the Reverend was right. Maybe it was time to turn the other cheek. He did not think the marriage could be saved, but at least he might salvage his dignity.

He was careful entering the apartment when he came in that afternoon. "Anna?" he called, to no reply. But where lurked Smitty? In what corner crouched the striped and splayfoot beast? Carey slid the box along the carpeted hall, peering in each doorway before he passed it. In the bathroom, the litter box brimmed with abstract figurines of desiccated shit, but the deceivingly unforked tail was nowhere to be seen.

In the nursery, he took all the pieces out of the box, was staring perplexedly at the instruction sheet and the little plastic bag of bolts when the phone rang. He answered in the bedroom. It was Pauline, his sister-in-law. Instantly, Carey became ticky and nervous. Pauline had his number, he was certain—maybe Anna had given it to her! She had his number, and now she was calling him.

He said, "Anna's not here. I think she's at your mother's."

"She is. I'm here, too, and I just found out that she hasn't had an ultrasound." There was a pause in which Carey assumed he was to offer an explanation for this outrageous admission. With none forthcoming, Pauline went on. "I mean, she's seven months pregnant and she hasn't had an ultrasound."

"She goes to a naturopath."

"That's what I just found out. A naturopath? Give me a break. You could have a baby with two heads. You realize that, don't you? Do you want a baby with two heads?"

"No," said Carey, sitting down on the bed. That would be a dead give-away. Nervously, he began tweaking at his glans through the fabric of his pants.

"Well?" Pauline demanded.

"Who's the father?" Carey blurted.

"Why do you all keep asking me that? It isn't funny anymore."

He hung up. Everything had changed colour in the room, the walls washed with a rosy hue as if he were squeezing a bulb that pumped blood to his eyes, tinting his vision. Then the overhead projector in his mind switched on and the little Sri Lankan girl in his class appeared before him stained, not red, but with the cosmetic yellow dye she sometimes used. His whole fist filled up, plenty rising out the top, too, so there was nothing the matter with him physically.

First Anna's belly came home, then, a full moment later, the rest of her. She was rubbing the small of her back and smiling to herself. When she saw him there, she looked taken aback. Carey, who made a point of never acknowledging the martyr-like pleasure she took in her discomfort, said nothing by way of greeting, merely continued planning his next day's lesson on the coffee-table.

"Maybe I'll take a bath before dinner," she told him.

She had to lumber past the nursery on her way to the bathroom, but did not look in. Carey heard the tub filling, then the taps shut off and the porcelain squeak complainingly as she lowered her bulk in. He got up and went to turn on the nursery light, pausing in the hall when he came out. The water swished and splashed in rhythm, then Anna's voice started up, resonant in the echo chamber of the bathroom, sounding like more than one singer, like two overlapping in the slow round of a lullaby. For a long time he stood transfixed.

The sound of scratching brought him to and he stepped away from the bathroom door. Following it to the source, he found that it was coming from the bottom cupboard in the kitchen where Anna kept the canned goods. He went over and grazed his fingernails across the wood. From inside came a frenzied reply in kind.

When Anna called to him, he went to her right away, found her in the nursery clutching around her a towel that would barely close. Staring at him with marvelling eyes, she gestured to the assembled crib sitting alone in the middle of the room. "Did you do this?"

He took all the credit. "Yes."

"Oh, Carey," she sighed.

Seeing she was about to cry, Carey opened up his arms. He started to, had just raised them to the level of his waist when Anna let out a little shriek. From between her thickened legs, something gushed. Instantly, the carpet sopped it up, but they both stood blinking down at the lily pad of wetness. "Was that pee?" Carey asked, disgusted.

"Archie gets up at 7.30." He pointed to the picture strip thrown against the wall by the overhead projector. "He takes a shower. He eats breakfast. He reads the paper." It was the kind of day Carey would have liked to have himself, the kind of life—in black and white, in present habitual, securely routine, devoid of surprises. "At 8.30, he drives to work. He starts work at nine o'clock." At no point in Archie's day did his wife's waters break because, unlike Carey, Archie didn't have a cartoon marriage.

A knock on the classroom door. Carey opened it to the security guard handing him a note and winking. The note said that Anna had gone to the hospital. He folded the paper in half and, slipping it in his shirt pocket, resumed teaching.

"At noon, he eats lunch in the cafeteria."

At noon, Carey went downstairs and ate his sandwich in the staffroom.

In the afternoon, the security guard came back with a note that this time asked him to phone the hospital. "It's an emergency."

His students were still barely able to chorus back the mundane events of Archie's day. Carey told the security guard, rather shortly, "I'm in the middle of a lesson."

After class, he did his photocopying for the next day and put his desk in order as it seemed likely that he would have to call a substitute. He wandered out to the parking-lot, then sat a long time in the car, as if trying to recall how to start it. "At four o'clock, Carey drives home," he said, turning on the ignition.

Two blocks from school, he passed a bus stop and saw from the corner of his eye the little Sri Lankan girl still waiting. "What would Archie do?" he asked himself as he looped around the block. Archie's inky hair never moved. He was entirely composed of lines. Archie, an affable smile penned across his face, would offer her a ride.

When he pulled up, it took the girl a moment to notice it was her teacher leaning across the passenger seat to open the door. "Rajeswary!" he called. Shyly, she came over jingling the little bells on the anklets she wore above her Nikes and giggling helplessly. "Your bus no coming," she sang.

"My bus," Carey corrected. "Where do you live? I'll drive you home." He patted the seat and grinned right at her bindi, which he had spent many a classroom hour surreptitiously eyeing. "What's your address?"

Climbing hesitantly into the car, she told him, painstakingly chanting it as he'd taught her.

"Do you live with your parents?" Carey asked as they drove off.

Her huge uncomprehending eyes turned to him.

"Your mother and your father."

"Oh," she said, frowning. "Your mother dead."

He received this news with a giddy, "What?" His mother *dead*?

"War," said Rajeswary. "Your mother dead."

Disappointment soured him and for several minutes they drove in silence, eastward, past muffler shops and dollar stores and produce markets. Finally, the girl spoke again. "Your baby?"

"My baby?" he said in a mocking tone. "My baby?"

"My baby!" she shrieked, embarrassed.

He had sunk into a funk, but she seemed not to understand it. "Your happy," she told him.

"Am I?" he shouted at her.

"Yes! Your father!"

He sneered.

"Your address," she whimpered.

"Here?" He stopped the car in front of a coin laundry where, on the second storey, apartment windows faced the street. Even after the frightened girl had bolted from the car, Carey sat there pounding his fist against the steering-wheel. He had racked his brain! Night after night he had lain awake trying to think of the men Anna knew who might be responsible, but he had not been able to think of anyone! With a screech he drove off homeward. Surely by now it would be over. Surely he wouldn't have to watch.

When he got in, the answering-machine was winking its red, accusing eye. There was a single, hissing message. "Asshole," Pauline said. "There is no heartbeat."

He went and stood in the nursery door, staring in at the crib in the centre of the otherwise empty room. Tucked-up inside it, a bolus of grey fur.

The tyrant was dying; she would not moon about to watch. Anna and her mother could stare at him in his cage of pain, but not Pauline. She got a stand-by flight to Acapulco and from there took the bus. Took buses. Often she was the only *gringa* on them. The men crowded around her, clicking and whistling like starlings. The only English phrase she heard was, "Hey, Blondie." At first she did not realize they meant her.

Almost immediately she found herself seduced. It was the fruit. The mango's hairy core as she sucked it reminded her of a Mound of Venus. So like the women's fallen breasts were the papaya, their seeds slippery, cum-coated. She bounced on the seat while the huge breasts of the peasant woman next to her, unrestrained by a brassière, moved in the same orgiastic rhythm. The dark oily faces of the men with their ripe lips began to excite rather than repel her. When she went up to the driver it was partly to feel their cockroach eyes scurrying across her body as she pitched and swayed in the aisle. She gestured for him to stop the bus: too much fruit, too much fruit! He understood and, though they were driving through forest, did not apply the brake until they had passed the sheltering trees and come to a mile of field. She clambered down and, with nowhere to go for privacy, squatted in the ditch. A hot flux gushed exquisitely from her. Glancing back at the bus windows lined with faces, she giggled.

Outside the depot in Oaxaca she bought strawberries for the last part of the trip. Their juice ran down her arms. Nothing to wipe it off with, she had to use her tongue. It was unseemly, she knew, a woman cleaning her arms like a predator after the kill. The men stared on, licking her with their eyes.

"You shouldn't eat those," someone across the aisle said. "You shouldn't eat anything that's not cooked or peeled."

She had thought he was Mexican, but now that he had given himself away, she noticed his pallor. His accent was American. "The weirdest goddam thing just happened to me," he told her, "so please don't eat those strawberries."

He had been working in the mountains on a development project, was heading back there now, though the way he was feeling, he wasn't sure he would make it. Eight months in poverty and isolation had not agreed with his bowels. He had lost weight steadily until the morning he knew he had to leave. Something wasn't right. "I had that, you know, gut feeling, ha ha." They got him on the Oaxaca bus, but he had to keep asking the driver to stop.

"I know, I know," said Pauline. "And everybody watched."

"I wondered what the hell could be coming out. I mean, I wasn't eating anything. There I was, hunkering. I looked and —whoa there! Whoa just a minute! A piece of my goddam intestine!"

"What?" cried Pauline, recoiling. "Coming out?"

"I was shitting out my guts."

"No way."

"Yeah. So I stuffed it back in and got back on the bus gripping my ass. Days it seemed to take to get to Oaxaca. Months. The whole time I sat there clenching."

"Oh, God," said Pauline. "Oh, my God."

"Finally, I got to the clinic. My guts are coming out! My guts are coming out! Crazy *gringo*. The doctor saw me right away. No rubber glove, nothing. Just stuffed his finger up my Khyber Pass. *Señor*, he said with perfect manners, I suggest you go right now to the toilet."

His white face sheening with sweat, he paused and stretched his lips in a slow, sick grimace.

"Are you okay now?" Pauline asked.

"It was as long as my arm. Jesus Christ. Have you ever *seen* a tapeworm?"

She got off the bus at Puerto Angel and from there had to walk, not on a road exactly, just a wide sandy path through the forested hills where the peasants drove their burros. Whenever she met a man he would, in a simultaneous gesture, avert his eyes and touch his hat brim. So unlike how they had treated her on the buses, either they feared her here or they hated her. She preferred the obscene chirrings because she understood them.

163

Rounding a bend and looking down, her first glimpse was of an irradiant half-circle of sand cupping turquoise water. Where she stayed there were no walls, only a palm-thatched roof supported by wooden posts—a house undressed, in effect. Everything was owned by Americans and most of the people were American, or German. The only time she ever saw a Mexican on that beach was very early one morning before anyone else had gotten up. He was utterly still, poised, something shiny in his hand. Walking toward him, she saw it was a machete, but had no time to feel afraid; as soon as he saw her coming, he turned and ran. When she reached the place he had been standing she noticed a few feet away a giant sea tortoise labouring, moving her clumsy flippers back and forth in the white sand, making an angel that would ease her down to a depth safe enough to lay her eggs.

The waves rolled onto the beach, then retreated in a rhythm as regular as a metronome set on largo. It was the very pace of life, the timing of those days. She rose early, took a walk, then climbed the hill to the café for breakfast. Afterward, she would lie on the sand reading a book she'd picked up somewhere. Maybe the story didn't interest her, or the sun was glaring off the page, but she found herself always reading the same six pages over and over again. She'd doze off, only to wake in time for a siesta and stagger back to her hammock under the leafy roof. For dinner there was beer, fried fish, fruit. It got dark early. Someone had a guitar and would play Dylan or The Eagles. The pot was excellent. The waves rolled up. The waves rolled back.

She had no idea how long she'd been there when she began to feel unwell. There was no way of telling time, no calendar or clock. Too much of an effort, carving notches in a tree. No-one had a mirror so she could not see if her hair had finally bleached enough to earn her the appellation "Blondie," or if the skin on her behind had darkened to a native shade. Her body offered no clues at all: since she had gone off the pill, her periods had ceased. Civilization's other chronometer, laundry day, did not apply.

"I ate some strawberries," she confessed when someone finally noticed she was ill. Apparently, it was common knowledge that the fields were irrigated with raw sewage. She mentioned the possibility of worms.

"Worms at least."

She should have gone back to Puerto Angel and found a doctor, but could not face the walk. Even getting from her hammock to the beach exhausted her. She would lie in a stupor on the sand, now and then digging a hole to retch in, thinking about her father who would be dead by now. Probably she was sun-stroked from lying there too long, delirious and therefore susceptible to weird imaginings. Her father had died, but that did not mean the end of their clash of wills. Far from it. Now he was inside her, fighting her from within.

Then one morning she woke feeling herself again, but very hungry. Overnight her energy had returned. Triumphantly, she climbed the hill to the café. The woman who worked there looked surprised to see her. "I haven't seen you for so long, I thought you'd split."

"How long?" asked Pauline.

The woman shrugged, guessing, "Six weeks?"

It had seemed a lot longer to Pauline who now felt silly for imagining the spirit of her father had possessed her in the guise of a tapeworm. She must have been hallucinating. In fact, she remembered she had eaten some mushrooms a few days before falling sick, so maybe the whole episode had been nothing more than a very long, very bad trip. She ordered a *cafe con leche* and pancakes. The woman sauntered over to the wood stove. Between her brown thighs, the string of a tampon dangled.

The waves rolled on. She sang "Tequila Sunrise" again and passed along the joint. Leaning back into the arms of some boy, she heard him whisper, *"Gorda,"* felt his tongue work through her tangled hair and probe her none-too-clean ear. Just then, in her belly, something lurched. She sat up, rose clumsily to her feet and hurried from their circle with the boy in tow.

"Que pasa?" he asked.

"Leave me alone."

"Is it because I called you fat?"

165

"Get lost," she told him. She could feel it coiling and un-coiling, nudging the walls of her gut, slithering through the folded corridors of intestine, trying doors. Pounding fists against her spongy, distended abdomen, she screamed, "Get lost!"

Putting on her clothes the next morning confirmed that she was bloated. Her shorts would not close. Thankfully, she had a drawstring skirt and a baggy shirt. Clutching her phrase-book, she left Paradise, not even wearing any panties.

There was no translation for "tapeworm," she discovered after arriving at the Puerto Angel clinic. "*Serpienta,*" she told the nurse, "*serpienta,*" and pointed to her bum.

"*Loca,*" she heard the nurse tell the doctor in the next room. "*Otra gringa loca.*"

"*Esta vestida?*" asked the doctor. They both laughed, then the nurse came back with a half dozen white suppository bullets that were, naturally, ineffective.

All her life Pauline had watched people watching her sister. She had seen their eyes shift focus the moment Anna came into the room and never really centre back on Pauline. They would look to Pauline again, certainly, but their eyes would be empty after that, gazing inwardly instead, at the lovely memory of Anna passing. Didn't Pauline want to claw at those eyes every time that happened? Didn't she just want to scream? It wasn't fair and neither was how Pauline was blamed for every fight between the sisters. So many weekends grounded for supposedly picking on Anna, the whole of Pauline's adolescence seemed to have been spent in the prison of her room. Of course, Pauline was also punished for the many outrageous things she did. She was known as an atten-tion-seeker, though attention wasn't half of what she sought. What she really wanted was to be adored, like Anna.

In Mexico, as she moved over the hot sand, stately, one—no, two—in a procession, everyone turned to follow her with their eyes. There were astonished double-takes, audible clucks of admiration. Strangers patted her belly, stroked it even, despite the nudist credo not to touch without permission. They would not let her be alone, not even for a second. If she

rose from her hammock and headed toward the waves, someone would instantly appear on either side to escort her in.
They took turns fanning her with palm fronds and once, while
she napped on the beach, someone sculpted her likeness in wet
sand three feet away. Waking, she marvelled at the belly of
the sand goddess beside her, the protruding navel a seashell
spiral. If only it could have lasted.

She came home before she got too big to fly. The next week
she had the ultrasound. "Look," said the technician, pressing
the lubricated wand hard under Pauline's ribs. On the screen,
the ghost of five little bean-shaped toes curled and uncurled.

"Great," drolled Pauline. "It has a foot." Nothing could
convince her that these separate parts would come out properly strung together. No way. Pauline had done way too many
drugs. She planned donations to the eye bank and the foot
repository after it was over.

"You don't want the baby?" asked the technician.

"I'm more of a cat person."

They offered her a picture, so she took the one of the foot
and brought it home to show her mother. Betty surprised her
by saying, "It's too bad your father couldn't see this."

"Why? He'd only ground me."

"He wouldn't have to. That baby's going to ground you.
You'd better believe it."

Pauline didn't. Nobody had ever really cramped her style
and a person weighing in at under ten pounds was, she
thought, an unlikely first.

"I'm dying!" she screamed. She was pushing a planet out her
loins in great shuddering, tearing waves. "I'm dying!" and
finally a head emerged, then a floppy sunburned body gooey
with silver vernix. Eyes slitty, but the mouth open wide.
Inside: white gums and a furred, thrushy tongue that would
soon send burning darts shooting up Pauline's milk ducts.
The greedy way she grabbed at the nipple the moment she
was placed on Pauline's chest, gave Pauline her first inkling as
to how things were going to be. They were going to be about
the baby. Already, the baby was shrieking: *me! me! me!*

They sent her home the next day. How to care for an infant,

Pauline had no idea; every time they had wheeled Rebecca into the room in her clear plastic box, Pauline had opened one eye and waved the nurse off as if refusing the fare on a dim sum trolley. She hadn't wanted to see anyone who could have used her so violently.

Once home, she hobbled around the house with a sopping, brick-thick menstrual pad between her legs, but no-one paid attention. "I have a hemorrhoid," she announced to Anna and Carey and Betty convening around the bassinet. Betty was concerned because Rebecca had changed colour and now looked washed in an iodine solution. All over her misshapen head, black hair was patched like a radiation victim's. Pauline lifted the hand mirror and examined again the catherine wheel of broken blood vessels in her left eye, from pushing. No-one had given her an ounce of sympathy for that either.

She'd had enough. She was going to head back to Mexico with her inheritance. Bow-legged, she pegged up the stairs, dressed, packed and left unnoticed. She thought she would call a cab from the grocery store on the corner, but when she had got halfway across the yard *Me! me! me!* came floating through the open window. *Me! me! me!* Panic overwhelmed her. She beat a stinging retreat and burst back in the house.

"Is she crying?" she called.

"Shh!" hissed Anna. "You're going to wake her up!"

In Pauline's nightmare she was watching herself sleep. For hour after decadently uninterrupted hour, she slept on because, for once, Rebecca was not shrilling. She watched herself toss dreamily in the covers, saw her own chest heave languorous sighs of relaxation and peace. The dream-Pauline was not the one having the nightmare. She was in a state of complete bliss.

Then, in the nightmare, the closed bedroom door opened up a crack. Someone was looking in at the dream-Pauline, but she did not know it. The door opened wider and a person stepped inside. For some reason the diminutive stature of the intruder was the most terrifying thing about her. She was an evil imp or dwarf or, worse—a child! Reminded then that there was a baby in the house, Pauline began to panic. Where was the baby? Why was she not waking every other hour? And who was this menacing little creature creeping over to the bed, tip-toeing closer and closer to her oblivious dreaming self? Had she done something to the baby? What? What?

Now it became apparent that it *was* a child, a child dressed up like a lamb. Still Pauline did not wake, not until the child was right beside her, glowering in her fleece hood, the ears pricked up. Abruptly, the dream-Pauline sat up, pulling the covers tight around her. Her mouth opened to scream, but no sound came out. Only the little girl could speak. Squishing up her nose, she grabbed Pauline's wrist so her nails dug in.

"Me-ow."

"I'm in labour!" sang Anna on the phone.

"Right," Pauline scoffed.

"I *am*!"

"It's false labour."

"My waters broke."

Pauline hesitated. After seven months of jealous waiting, she was unwilling to let her hopes rise, especially prematurely like this. "Any contractions?"

"What do they feel like?"

Pauline laughed. "Call me back."

The day before the sisters had gone for lunch. Two men in business suits, allowed now to perform all the chivalrous gestures banned by feminism, rushed to open the door for Anna. They followed her solicitously into the restaurant, leaving Pauline outside grappling with a toddler, the full set of luggage that came with her—diaper bag, toy bag, food bag, stroller—and now the door. Pauline nearly spat. How she longed for that commanding, dirigible figure herself! She wanted to feel once again inflated with her own euphoria.

Rebecca was in the bathroom unspooling toilet paper all over the floor. "Auntie Anna's going to have a baby. Baby's coming." She scooped up her child, hot sticky cheek against her dry one and, simultaneously, a cool seashell ear. "Poor Auntie Anna," she laughed. Soon she would be as enslaved by a tiny pair of screw-on hands creased at the wrists, by a round tyrant face peering out from under a KKK-hooded bath towel. Unbidden and unstoppable, the love would pour out of her like milk.

Anna didn't call back until the next morning when she was about to leave for the hospital. Pauline said she would meet her there. By cab, she took Rebecca to her mother's where, parting, she grabbed her dirty hand, kissed it fervently, then pushed it right inside her mouth, pretending to eat it. Rebecca shrieked delightedly. *If anything happens to you,* Pauline incanted in her head, *I will kill myself by the slowest, most agonizing method. I will stick pins in my every pore. I will gargle battery acid.*

Anna had just been relegated a curtained cubicle and gown when Pauline got there. "Where's Carey?"

"He's working," said Anna. "But he'll come. I know he will."

"If you've actually got a father, he may as well be here."

Anna bowed her head and, gripping the chrome rails at the sides of the bed, panted heavily. When she lifted her face again, Pauline saw how bloated she was, her pretty features embedded in flushed and sweating cheeks. "I feel like pushing," she gasped.

"What? Already?" Pauline hurried off to get a nurse.

The nurse came back with Pauline and did the internal examination while Pauline stayed by the head of the bed. "You're not the teeniest bit dilated," she told Anna, straightening and peeling off the rubber glove. "I'm going to send you home."

"No!" cried Anna. "The baby's coming!"

"That may be," said the nurse, "but it's not coming soon."

"I won't go home! I won't!" She flopped sideways on the bed and curled up fetal, hiding her face so it was hard to tell if she was crying or puffing through another contraction. The hospital gown stretched open between the ties and Pauline looked away.

The nurse said, "You'll be more comfortable at home."

"We can go to Ma's," Pauline suggested.

"No!"

The nurse turned to Pauline. "I'll get the resident to come and see her."

As soon as she had gone, Anna asked plaintively, "Paulie?

How bad is it going to get?"

"Awful," Pauline chirped.

Anna reached for her hand and, embarrassed, Pauline gave it to her and let her squeeze it. She was still sitting on the edge of the bed with Anna gripping her when the resident finally came in. He was not bad looking, blond with wire-framed glasses, but Pauline decided—nobly, she thought—that this was not the time. He asked Anna to roll over onto her back and, with her permission, lifted the gown. He had brought a fetal heart monitor which he placed on one side of Anna's tummy. Immediately, it broadcast her digestive rumblings across the room. He moved it around: more under-water churnings. Pauline was staring at Anna's navel, which had not popped, but was instead a deep hole with no visible bottom. When she looked up, she saw the resident had fixed on her a look so sobering that she no longer found him remotely attractive.

"I have a phone call to make," she announced, wresting her hand from Anna's, hoping she didn't sound too panicky. "I'll be back in a second."

Leaving through the slit in the curtains, she walked quickly past the nursing-station. What she was thinking was how, when she had first got back from Mexico, her mother had accused her of having no conscience. "Your father died without being able to tell you goodbye. Couldn't you even have called?" Taking umbrage at the accusation, Pauline had retorted, "There wasn't a phone!" No-one understood that it was out of respect for Robert that she had stayed away.

She found the bathroom and, once inside, immediately began to sob. Remorse gushed out of her—her!—former perpetrator of so many childhood atrocities, outlandish denier of them. She used to bury Anna dolls in the garden, marking the spot with a cross made out of sticks. As soon as Anna discovered one missing, she would run shrieking into the yard to find the grave and disinter it. Once, the night before school pictures, Pauline cut off one of Anna's braids. Though Anna always went to Robert demanding justice, Pauline stubbornly refused to acknowledge her guilt. The golden snake of Anna's braid in her own wastebasket, still Pauline would clamp her jaws tight, refusing to confess. Yet she *had* done those things and, sobbing over the sink, she couldn't shake the hideous feeling that she was also at fault for whatever had gone wrong with Anna's baby though it was a tragedy she would not have wished even on her worst enemy.

As soon as she had pulled herself together, she went to phone Betty. "Ma," was all she managed to say. "Oh, Ma."

"Has something happened?"

"Ma, it's dead."

Pauline had never known her mother to cry. What she heard now, once she finally managed to quiet herself, was a pause, a metallic rasp and click, an inhalation, then the quiet pop of the filter released.

"I better phone Carey."

"Isn't he there?" Betty exclaimed.

Pauline left a message for him at home. Looking in the phone book for the school where he worked, none of the names sounded familiar. She went to the gift shop for more quarters, then called around until she found the right place. When she got back to the ward, she couldn't seem to find Anna's cubicle. Disoriented, she looked in one, then the next, but every curtain she looked behind showed a different woman labouring. It felt nightmarish and, frantic now, she returned to the nursing-station just as the nurse who had done the internal examination appeared from around the corner.

"They're taking your sister upstairs," she said, gesturing down the corridor.

"What about the baby?" cried Pauline.

"What?"

"The baby!"

"Didn't the resident speak with you?"

"No."

"You'd better go with her."

"Where are they taking her?"

"Up to Psychiatry. You can catch up. Go."

Pauline ran and, turning at the end of the corridor, saw a stretcher being wheeled into the elevator. She sprinted and stopped the door just in time. Anna was sobbing on the stretcher while the other people in the elevator, the orderly, a man on crutches and a couple bearing flowers, looked down at her with pity and concern.

"What's going on?" Pauline demanded.

Anna only sobbed louder.

"Tell me what is going on!"

Anna was hysterical. "They won't let me have my baby!"

Pauline reached out suddenly, her fingers sinking into fat, Anna's belly yielding passively to the jab. "Oh you!" she cried, incensed. Without even thinking, she brisked her knuckles hard across Anna's forehead.

"Ow!" shrieked Anna, bringing up her hands.

"Hey, hey!" said the man on crutches. The orderly tried to grab Pauline's arm, but she got one last noogie in before the elevator door opened. Bursting out, nearly colliding with a wheelchair, she flew off down the hall. Light on her feet—unlike Anna!—she skipped to dodge a cart, laughed. "Whoops!" The taste of sorry had completely left her mouth.

So Beautiful the Firemen Would Cry

Ramona Dearing

I started keeping my toothbrush in my underwear drawer after Beanie told me what she did to her last roommate. She wanted to make sure I understood it was a very unusual thing for her to do and that she'd been extremely provoked along the lines of her bitch ex-roommate being two months behind on the rent and always eating Beanie's butter and then swearing innocence. I appreciated having the context, but it's still a little uncomfortable knowing the person you're sharing an apartment with used to twirl their old roommate's toothbrush in the toilet twice every day—first thing in the morning, and also after Beanie's last pee at night.

When she told me about it, Beanie said I must think she was terrible and I said, no, I kind of understood. But really, all I could see was that toothbrush going into the toilet twice a day and into a mouth twice a day.

After that, I kept an old toothbrush as a decoy in the holder, just left it there and never used it. Sometimes it seemed a little damp, but I'd have to wash my hands four times to get rid of any germs after touching it so after a while I stopped checking. Also, suspicion on that level kills something inside you eventually, which is why I decided to cool it.

One time she almost caught me. I was in my robe, getting ready to crash. I was going to do one of those round trips—you know, go to the kitchen for a glass of water and then to the bathroom to wash my face before crawling into bed. I'd set the non-decoy toothbrush down on the counter. Just then Beanie came home and stuck her head in the kitchen door to say hi. After that, I kept the toothbrush under my pillow, wrapped in Saran Wrap, because I thought she might come looking for it and the drawer was kind of obvious. But like I said, what's the point of living like that? After a couple of weeks, I made myself put it back in the bureau.

Most times Beanie was an excellent person to live with. We had all this stuff in common: both of us were new to Vancouver and couldn't really get a grip on the place, and both of us were single. But it was more than just the big stuff. Beanie's the only other person I've ever met who eats popcorn with a spoon. Also, she used to read Baba Yaga stories when she was a kid, just like I did. And, weirdest of all, we both had aunts in Bathurst, New Brunswick.

We used to clean together, if you can believe it. We liked that—music going, a pot of chai on the stove, everything in its place all shined up. We were forever rearranging the furniture because our living-room was about six inches square and we were determined to find a way to make it look bigger. But even with a white slipcover on the couch and a lick of white paint, the place still looked like a storage closet with a couch in it. We did a lot of this stuff on Saturday nights because we didn't have any friends. That was the thing about the city we couldn't figure. People would chat to me at the bus stop, or at the very least smile. And at school—which is why I was in Vancouver—everyone was nice, nice, nice, but I'd still go home on the bus right after class. Beanie had the same problem, even though she worked in a futon store, which you'd think would be a cozy place to develop inter-employee relations.

Whoever got home first would cook and make enough for the other person. That was usually me, and then Beanie would do the dishes. It was pleasant, you know. Our dining-room was really a little balcony that had been glassed in. We could feel squirrel holes under the linoleum, but if the rain stopped we could see the mountains. Once I saw a coyote on the grass out front, and then a couple of days later I saw a guy standing in that exact same spot, shooting up.

It was pretty safe where we lived, which was in the east end, near Commercial Drive, although there was a crack house right around the corner. One time when I walked past, a man pushed another man down the porch steps while a woman whipped the falling guy with a rope. The rule with that kind of situation in Vancouver is not to make eye contact, just keep looking straight ahead. But coming in from Fredericton like I did, it took a while to figure that out. I remember this crazy guy downtown on a Sunday when I was walking to the Stadium Skytrain station. I looked right at him because I didn't want him to think that I thought he was crazy and he came at me with his arm out and his hand in a fist and said, "You want a punch, you ugly fucking cow?"

In a way, that was my welcome to Vancouver, because it happened right after I arrived. So it was good to have Beanie around. She'd come in from Toronto, but she was even more disturbed by the city than I was because she'd decided Vancouver was where she was going to spend the rest of her days. I was going back to Fredericton to do my Ph.D. in English so I could live with my parents and save money. Beanie was living her dream of being in a big city that had mountains and sushi and beaches and monkey trees. She thought Vancouver was ahead of its time. She was proud that to get home from work, she'd catch the bus in front of this fetish shop called Cabbages & Kinx and then she'd hop off right outside the women's sex shop on the Drive, which had a mural featuring butt plugs and vibrators and dildos kind of doing a happy dance together (picture that in Fredericton!). But it did bother Beanie, going through the downtown eastside. She told me that once she saw a sixteen-year-old who looked like she should be eating strawberry shortcake and wearing headphones, but instead was rocking back and forth on the sidewalk in the rain, no coat.

You could see it surprised Beanie, the suffering she saw in Vancouver. She came home one night and said she'd just walked past nine people begging on the Drive and hadn't given any of them anything. She wanted to know what it did to you inside to keep walking past them, what it would do to you after ten years. I said just fork out extra rent money and move to Kits, like everyone else. She said there were lots of street people in Toronto but that they weren't all so young and didn't shoot up right in front of you.

They didn't do that in Fredericton, either, since no-one lives on the streets. Saturday market is about as exciting as the place gets, or maybe the first thaw on the river.

Beanie said she needed a break and that I did, too. We'd heard Bowen Island was a funky place. We decided to go on the next sunny or semi-sunny Sunday or Monday because those were Beanie's days off. But it was November. We counted eighteen straight days of rain, and then I said we'd better stop counting for our mental health.

So Beanie told me to wake her up early enough to call in sick on the next sunny day, and I said sure. But I was lying, because I have this thing which is something like a phobia about not waking people up. I don't know why, but it makes me feel sick. There were a couple of okay mornings where they said on the radio it would be fairly dry that day, but I didn't go and get Beanie because of what I already told you.

One morning—I think it was December by then—Beanie slapped my door and said, "Let's do it." It was 8.30 and there was enough light coming in through my curtains that I could see the corners of my room for a change. I could smell bacon and coffee. She did my eggs over easy for me and said she'd already called work. It was a Thursday. I was supposed to hand in a paper on Robert Kroetsch that Monday coming and hadn't started on it, because that's the way I am. I said I couldn't go, but she got huffy and I remembered the tooth-brush story and wondered if I should provoke her.

We took the bus to Horseshoe Bay, and everyone waiting was in a good, good mood. A sunny day in Vancouver is kind of like a full moon in some other places: it sure changes people. The ferry ride was nice—short, but still we could see the coast mountains and also one stretch of water out past the islands where it's just pure Pacific. No coves or inlets, just calm water stretching out forever.

Put a rain forest on an island in one of the rainiest spots in the rain forest zone, and you get Bowen Island. We got onto the hiking trail straight off, where the moss on the trees was unbelievably green. If it was a paint colour, I'd call it "Spanky Leprechaun." There were ferns the size of nightmares running alongside the trail, and ravens screaming from the trees instead of monkeys. Our sneakers went right down into the mud. It felt to me like a place that was so alive that it was almost choking itself. Even the dead stumps of trees kept growing—moss spilled right out of them.

I had an inclination to find a meadow and stay there, but Beanie loved the woods. "Smell that?" she kept saying. "I'd put a cabin exactly here."

It started to rain pretty hard, which made me a little more inclined to like rain forests since all that greenery acts like a leaky umbrella. It was Beanie's idea to get off the trail and onto this road we could see running close by. She figured we could hitchhike, or that at least it would be a shorter walk back to Snug Cove and the ferry terminal. It was a dirt road and it kept forking into other dirt roads, so I knew we were probably walking away from the ferry landing instead of toward it. We walked past someone's tipi, but it didn't seem like there was anybody home. Same with a yurt. We were pretty wet and cold, but all the hippie stuff made us giddy—I mean, you hear people talk about how loopy BC is, but you think it's an exaggeration. We decided some woman named Kiki lived in the tipi, and that a guy named Kurt had the yurt.

Then we came to another fork in the road, except this time there was a rope across it and a sign saying visitors were welcome as long as they didn't let the horses out. There was a little gold Buddha sitting on top of a tree trunk, and next to it was another sign with an arrow underneath the word "Labyrinth."

So of course we ducked under the rope and followed the arrow. There were all these little plaster cherubs and gnomes along the sides of the path. They looked extra white against all the dank and green and they scared me. Beanie was loving it, though. "We are adventuring," she said, "and I moved here exactly because deep inside I am an adventuring babe."

The labyrinth was in a small meadow, which calmed me down a bit. Someone had painted all these rocks white and used them to make the design. We stepped inside and started going around and around.

It was one of those prayer mazes—you know, all paths lead to God. After maybe ten minutes, I stepped outside the rock border. Going around and around was just too boring, and also a lot of extra walking; I wanted to save my strength for figuring out where we were.

But Beanie kept going. She hopped along on one leg for a while and then switched to the other. "Kiki's tipi," she said. "Kurt's yurt."

We were both laughing. "Hurry up," I said.

When she got to the centre, she dropped down on her knees. "Wow," she said. "Big whoop." But she stayed there for a few minutes before getting up. "That's better," she said.

As soon as we got back to the road, a pickup went by. We flagged it down and got a lift right down to the ferry dock. There was a boat waiting, too, but we decided to get some fish and chips and catch another sailing. Even with all the grease, I could feel the beer buzzing in my blood. It made me wish I was there with a real friend, not just a circumstantial one.

Beanie told me that when she'd sat there in the middle of the labyrinth, she heard the same word running around and around in her head. She figured it had been going around like that for a long time, like one of those whirligig lawn ornaments that look like the guy's legs are moving because the winds spins them around.

My socks were wet and the pub was cold. "Come on," I said, "we've got four minutes to get to down there if we're going to get the next ferry."

"I don't feel like rushing," she said. "I'm too full to run."

I decided it was her call, since the whole trip was her idea.

"So, anyway, yeah, this word was 'trust,' that's what was going around and around in there and I wasn't hearing it, you know?"

"Like literally? An actual word being said out loud in your head?"

"So I'm thinking I should tell you this thing which I've never told anyone."

I didn't want to hear it. No matter what she said, it was going to affect me. Like that toothbrush story, only this one would be bigger, obviously. And it didn't matter what she

179

said—whether she was pregnant or had HIV or got fired or was coming out of the closet—it was going to change my life.

She told me she'd tried to do herself in about three months before moving to Vancouver. She loved this guy Todd and they lived together but then he came home one night and said it wasn't working but that they'd be friends forever, wouldn't they? And she found out where he was and started phone-stalking him and then he got unlisted so she took some pills and put on this dark green silk nightgown number with a V-neck and lace straps and got into bed with the pillows just so and her hair just so because she wanted to look so beautiful the firemen would cry when they had to come and put her body on the stretcher.

But she barfed up the pills and didn't even go to the doctor's the next day because it only felt like a really bad hangover. She didn't tell anyone, even though she had a roommate, the toothbrush one.

"So, you know, how's everything going now?" I said after she'd gotten into the mechanics of suicide for a while and how hard it is to die because your body wants to live no matter how crap-plugged your mind is.

She said not to worry, that she felt great. That she was making all these little steps forward and that she knew Vancouver would be really good for her once she got used to it.

I asked if she'd done the counselling thing and she told me she didn't believe in stirring up the pot when it wasn't necessary and that she knew first-hand from when she was fourteen and her mom sent her to a shrink that counsellors like to keep everything edgy because it's more interesting for them. "I mean, you must know about that," she said.

I told her I'd never gone to a professional.

"But you've tried the other solution, right? Everyone has at some point."

I've always kind of liked being alive, but I didn't want to say that and make her feel bad. "I've had some crappy times."

"So how?"

"Huh?"

"Which way did you try?"

I could see this excitement on her face as she waited for me to answer. "You've never?"

I shook my head.

"Wow," she said, "you really are weird."

After that I worried for about a month. I kept thinking that Beanie was dead in her room, with the blankets cuffed nicely, her whole torso propped up on pillows, her hands folded, her skin damp and cold under that green nightdress.

Then Beanie met Frank. He had these eyes that could knock you over. She was happy, all right. They went out to the Railway Club and the W.I.S.E. hall and to the tapas bar on the Drive where this band played funky flamenco music. She cut a couple of sarong skirts out of batik fabric and wore them with a little white blouse tied in a knot at her belly button. She laughed a lot.

I was only jealous maybe ten or fifteen times, right at the beginning. I just felt kind of ugly and lonely, although it's not like I wanted Frank. He worked as a hand on a tugboat and I always knew if he was over as soon as I unlocked the door to the apartment because I'd either smell his sweat if he'd just gotten off shift or his Lysol-strength cologne if he was taking Beanie out somewhere. He said he figured he and Beanie were destined for each other, what with their names being Frank and Beanie, which he said you could boil down to Weenie and Beanie. "Get it?" he'd say. "Boil down. Get it?"

When Frank was stoned, he was useless. "What time are we going again?" he'd yell out to Beanie, who would plant him in the living-room while she got ready in her room.

"I said, we'll leave at 9.30."

"Oh," he'd say. Then after a few minutes, "What time did you say, hon?"

He'd do that lying on the couch with his shoes planted straight down on the slipcover. Sometimes he'd fall asleep and would snore, which made me want to scream since I'd be in the kitchen maybe seven feet away trying to cook something for myself. What really pissed me off was that I'd actually try not to make much noise, because you know how I am about waking people up. But one night I dropped a can of tomatoes on the floor on purpose. That gave him a jolt, all right. His feet flew off the couch and landed on the floor. I felt so bad I said, "Sorry," and then hated myself for being weak.

Each time Frank came over, he stayed longer. After about three weeks it was like he lived there. I came home one afternoon, and he had this jigsaw puzzle spread out on the dining-room table. It was supposed to be Van Gogh's self-portrait. Frank said he got it at Value Village and that he was going to put it together and glue it to some cardboard backing and then hang it on the wall. He said his friends would be impressed to see famous artwork at his place. But the thing was a bugger because each piece of the puzzle had these grids with tiny photographs of trucks and birds and stuff inside, to make it that much harder to do.

That jigsaw puzzle stayed on the table, which really was my table, for a week, about one-tenth done. I ate in my bedroom that whole time and thought about how good life would be without Frankenstein. What I did, finally, was vacuum every single stupid piece of that puzzle off the table. My alibi was going to be that I'd spilled a bowl of chicken noodle soup over the pieces by accident.

But I never got my chance—Frank disappeared. No phone call, no note, no nothing. At first Beanie was furious and then she got all worried that he'd drowned off the tug. Then she started crying all the time. I mean, all the time. She still went to work, so that was a good sign. But I'd call her for supper and she wouldn't come out of her room. I even made manicotti one night because she was wild for it, but she said sorry, she wasn't hungry. At night, I could hear her blowing her nose.

That Saturday when she came in from the Futon Factory, I caught her in the hallway before she could slide into her room. "You okay?" I said.

She thought for a long time. Then she said, "As well as can be expected."

"Want a hug or anything?"

She shook her head and took a couple of steps toward her room. "Come on," I said, and I gave her a geeky hug that she twirled right out of.

"Don't worry, I'm not mental," she said before she closed

her door. "In fact, I'm very clear at the moment."

That really scared me. You get really calm just before you do it, right? I almost called one of those hotlines, but I decided to keep monitoring for the next couple of days.

On her days off, Sunday and Monday, she was a shut-in. But I could hear her clearing her throat or walking out to the bathroom. I put a jug of water outside her door and a glass but I didn't knock in case she was sleeping. When I came back from the supermarket, they were gone. So I made a cheese sandwich and left that out there.

I got up really late on Tuesday because I'd forced myself to make some headway on my paper on Ondaatje's *Running in the Family*. It was such a good read I almost hated to mess it up with an essay. Anyway, half the sandwich was gone. I didn't know if Beanie was at work or not.

When I got back from class, the half-sandwich was still there. It was 6.30 PM. I took the plate away and there was no light coming through the crack in the door. I had to do something. By 9.30, I knew she was dead and I was pretty sure I was going to be sick. I was wondering if I could touch her but I knew I couldn't—I've never touched a dead thing.

I put the bottom of my sweatshirt over her doorknob so I wouldn't leave any prints that would lead the cops to believe it was murder. I kept my hand on the doorknob for a long time. Finally, I started pushing the door open.

"Beanie?" I called. "Lucinda?" Which was her real name but she didn't like it because it reminded her of her childhood. "Beans? You have to get up."

Nothing. I stood really still and after a while I could hear her breathe. I wanted her to sit up on her own, without me saying another word. I don't know why it bothers me so much, waking people up. It scares me the same way all that swamp on Bowen Island scared me. But I had to do it— Beanie needed help, and I was going to make her go through her address book and pick out three people and make her promise to talk to them about what Frank did.

I went over to her bed and put my hand on her cheek, really slowly. Her legs slid around a bit and I could see her eyes open.

"I'm sorry I touched you and I'm sorry I woke you up." These slider tears were dropping right out of me, the kind that wet your whole face and roll under your chin.

"Hey," she said, patting my hand a couple of times.

"Look at you," I said. She'd been crying so much there was hardly any eyeball showing through all the puffiness. "Do you have your plans, you know, made?"

She sat up then and told me she would never, ever do anything like that to me—understood?

I said, "But your old roommate, she would have found you that time."

"First of all, that was not a smart thing. And second, this is friends here, okay?"

That just busted me, and then she started in, too. After a while I said, "You want me to pour you a bath?"

She nodded. "I know, I know, I'm going to have to talk to someone. In a few weeks or something."

I Ajaxed the tub for her and made sure to do a good job rinsing the grit out. I splashed my face with water in the sink and that's when I saw the decoy toothbrush. I grabbed it and put this careful, perfect line of toothpaste on it. And you know, I almost brushed my teeth. Except I couldn't. What I actually did was chuck that thing into the trash.

MICHAEL WINTER is the author of the story collection *One Last Good Look*, which was broadcast on CBC Radio, and a fictional journal, *This All Happened*. He divides his time between Toronto and St. John's, Newfoundland, where he is a member of the writers group The Burning Rock, with Lisa Moore, Ramona Dearing and Lawrence Mathews.

DON MCNEILL was born and raised in Newfoundland, but left to see the world and win Emmys for his journalism. Ten years ago he stopped travelling and began to write stories. He has appeared in *Coming Attractions* and published a collection of short fiction, *Submariner's Moon*.

ALICE MUNRO is one of Canada's best-known writers. Her most recent book of stories is *Hateship, Friendship, Courtship, Loveship, Marriage*. Many of her stories, like "Family Furnishings," have first appeared in *The New Yorker*. Alice Munro lives with her husband in a small town in southern Ontario.

MARK ANTHONY JARMAN is the author of *Salvage King Ya!*, *New Orleans is Sinking*, *19 Knives* and *Ireland's Eye*. In 2002 he received a Gold Medal from the National Magazine Awards Foundation and was a co-winner of the *Prism international* Short Fiction Contest. He is the fiction editor of *Fiddlehead* and teaches at the University of New Brunswick.

CAROL WINDLEY has published a novel, *Breathing Under Water*, and a collection of stories, *Visible Light*, that was nominated for the Governor General's Award. Her work has appeared in *Event*, *Descant*, *Malahat Review* and *Best Canadian Stories*. She lives in Nanaimo.

BERNICE FRIESEN has published fiction and poetry in such periodicals as *Malahat Review*, *Capilano Review* and *Canadian Literature*. A first collection of stories, *The Seasons are Horses*, appeared in 1995, and a collection of poetry, *Sex, Death, and Naked Men*, in 1998. She lives in BC and Saskatchewan.

P.K. PAGE is the author of more than fifteen books of poetry, fiction and non-fiction. *Planet Earth*, a volume of her selected poems, was published in the fall of 2002. Under the name of P.K. Irwin, her paintings appear in a number of collections including the Art Gallery of Ontario and the National Gallery of Canada.

BILL GASTON has lived and worked in Winnipeg, Toronto, Vancouver and the Maritimes, and currently teaches at the University of Victoria. He has published four novels, three books of short fiction and a collection of poetry, produced several plays and won the CBC Literary Award. "Comedian Tire" appears in his new collection from Raincoast Books, *Mount Appetite*.

CAROLINE ADDERSON is the author of *Bad Imaginings*, a first collection of stories that won the Ethel Wilson Fiction Prize and was nominated for the Commonwealth Book Prize and the Governor General's Award. Her novel *A History of Forgetting* was published in Canada in 1999 and in the UK in 2001.

RAMONA DEARING lives in St. John's, Newfoundland. Her poems and short fiction have appeared in periodicals including *Fiddlehead*, *Malahat Review*, *Grain* and *Prairie Fire*, and her stories have been published both in *Coming Attractions* and in previous editions of *Best Canadian Stories*.

DOUGLAS GLOVER is the author of four story collections and three novels, including the critically acclaimed *The Life and Times of Captain N*, as well as a collection of essays, *Notes Home from a Prodigal Son*. His stories have appeared in *Best American Short Stories*, *Best Canadian Stories* and *The New Oxford Book of Canadian Stories*, and criticism has appeared in the *Globe and Mail*, *Montreal Gazette*, *New York Times Book Review*, *Washington Post Book World* and *Los Angeles Times*. His most recent collection of stories is *16 Categories of Desire*, and a novel, *Elle*, will be published in 2003.